Friends
with Benefits

LENA MATTHEWS   MAGGIE
MATTHEWS   CASPER

ELLORA'S CAVE
ROMANTICA PUBLISHING

*W*hat the critics are saying...

೫೦

"In this sequel to *Maverick's Black Cat*, the world of BDSM is once again interestingly portrayed. The heroine is likable, and her developing interest and acceptance of the hero's sexual proclivities is nicely done." ~ *Romanctic Times Reviews*

5 Angels "*Friends with Benefits* is a fun, erotic book that I was not able to put down! Bailey and Sebastian make a wonderful couple that shoot sparks off of one another. This is the second book in this series, but can be read alone. *Maverick's Black Cat* was the first and is a great book also. I would suggest reading *Maverick's Black Cat* first where you will meet Cat and Mason who are Bailey and Sebastian's best friends and that is how the two meet. […] Some of the situations between the two are just fun as each wants to control the relationship. I thoroughly enjoyed this book and look forward to the next book from Ms. Casper and Ms. Matthews." ~ *Fallen Angel Reviews*

An Ellora's Cave Romantica Publication

www.ellorascave.com

Friends with Benefits

ISBN 9781419959257
ALL RIGHTS RESERVED.
Friends with Benefits Copyright © 2006 Maggie Casper & Lena
Matthews
Edited by Mary Moran.
Cover art by Willo.

This book printed in the U.S.A. by Jasmine-Jade Enterprises,
LLC.

Electronic book Publication November 2006
Trade paperback Publication July 2009

FRIENDS WITH BENEFITS

§

Trademarks Acknowledgement

The author acknowledges the trademarked status and trademark owners of the following wordmarks mentioned in this work of fiction:

Cheerios: General Mills IP Holdings I, LLC

Disney: The Walt Disney Company

H&R Block: H&R Block, Inc.

The Three Stooges: Comedy III Productions, Inc

Chapter One

ဆာ

Thirty-five. Thirty-six. Thirty-seven. The seconds seemed to take on a life all their own. Unfortunately for Bailey Edwards, they had taken on the life of a geriatric gout patient. The day was dragging by and slowly pulling her along, kicking and screaming, for the ride.

Then the clock struck one and all the tension that had built up in her shoulders flowed free. It was lunchtime.

The usually quiet office began to come alive as the accountants began to shuffle around. Apparently Bailey wasn't the only person doing a countdown. Before the large hand had fully clicked into its upright position, wheels squealed back across the floor as people rose from their desks.

The only thing better than quitting time was lunchtime.

Before Bailey could begin to relish in the pleasure of the break, a voice boomed from behind her, "Not going out to lunch today?"

With an insincere smile placed firmly on her lips, Bailey looked up at her coworker Hillary Tinell and tried to be polite. It was a difficult task though, because she truly hated the woman. "Not today. I have other plans."

"Other plans, huh?" Hillary smirked as she shot a knowing look in the direction of their supervisor's office. Her not so subtle meaning wasn't lost on Bailey. Neither were any of the other backhanded comments the woman had thrown her way.

"Yes, I have a lunch date."

"I'm sure you do." The smug tone of Hillary's voice set Bailey's nerves on edge and it took everything in her to allow the brunette to have the last word.

They were the only two black women who worked at Blum & Associates, which for that reason alone should have given them a small mound of common ground, but it didn't. Just further proving race had very little to do with compatibility.

One of these days she was going to knock the dread-wearing bimbo's capped teeth down her throat. Just when she found a job she enjoyed, with a boss who didn't chase her around the room or make lewd comments, Bailey was forced to deal with petty coworkers.

Once again, Bailey berated herself for quitting Broderick Inc. At the time it had seemed as if it were the right thing to do. She didn't want people to think she would get special privileges now that her best friend was married to the owner, but looking back on it, Bailey should have just stayed where she was.

If it wasn't one thing, it was surely another.

Bailey waited until everyone who was leaving the office left before she retrieved her briefcase from the bottom drawer of her desk and pulled out her laptop. The few stragglers who were left wouldn't bother her. They were either too busy working through lunch or nose-deep in a book. Just the company she was looking for.

After turning on her baby, Bailey took out the sandwich she had stored in her bag and waited for her laptop to come on. Wireless Internet was the brainchild of a god. Sometimes just knowing she could boot up and escape into cyber land was the only thing carrying her through the day.

Readying her desk for her lunch date, Bailey got comfortable as she turned on her messenger.

BlackCat: You're late.

The instant message box popped up not even two seconds after she logged in. Great. Her lunch date was right on time.

MsThang: Don't you have anything better to do than hang out on the computer?

BlackCat: I'm working.

MsThang: So does this mean you're having cyber sex with Mr. BlackCat? Should I IM you later?

Bailey chuckled out loud when the raised brow smiley icon popped on screen.

BlackCat: Shut up.

MsThang: I just don't want to interrupt your afternoon delight.

BlackCat: Are you ever going to let me live that down?

MsThang: Not a chance.

BlackCat: LOL I didn't think so.

As Catarena's best friend, it was Bailey's sworn duty to tease her about how she'd met her husband Mason Broderick. On some twisted porn level, their "how they met" love story was romantic.

Poor girl meets rich boy on jerk site. Boy dominates girl. Girl finds out boy is her boss. Boy and girl live happily ever after.

If Bailey hadn't been along for the ride, she would have never thought it possible. But it was. True love did exist, even if it didn't start off on the smoothest of paths.

BlackCat: Moving on, I want to hear about your date last night. I want everything from the nitty to the gritty.

Bailey smiled. Although she and Cat no longer shared an apartment, they still acted like gossiping schoolgirls whenever they got together, be it in cyber land or in one of their living rooms.

Their continuing friendship was one of the many things keeping Bailey afloat, especially after dates like the one she'd had last night.

MsThang: I'm never going to have sex again.

BlackCat: I take it Bill wasn't Mr. Right?

That was putting it lightly.

MsThang: He's not even good enough to be Mr. Right Now.

BlackCat: The date was that bad?

Unwrapping her sandwich, Bailey tried to think of a way to explain how the word "bad" was an understatement. A year ago it would have been a breeze to describe to Cat why the date had been awful, but then again, a year ago Cat had been single as well and not blinded by love.

MsThang: Let's just say if my dates keep going this badly, the next time I have sex will be online. But knowing my luck, I won't end up with my own version of "Million Dollar Mason".

BlackCat: * grin* You know Mason hates it when you call him that.

MsThang: So! He's not the boss of me anymore. Now he's just your boss.

BlackCat: And I love every second of it.

Although Bailey knew Cat couldn't see her face, she couldn't help but stick her tongue out. The last thing she wanted to hear right now was how satisfying her best friend's sex life was. There was only so much crap she could put up with for the sake of friendship and Cat's sexual bliss wasn't one of them.

MsThang: I think I'm going to give up men.

BlackCat: How often have I heard this?

MsThang: This time I mean it. Besides, I've been thinking.

BlackCat: Uh-oh. This isn't going to end well.

Ignoring Cat's comment, Bailey forged on.

MsThang: I think my main problem is I've been going out with the wrong type of men.

BlackCat: I could have told you that. In fact, I think I have told you that. Countless times if I recall correctly.

The only thing worse than hearing "I told you so" was knowing the person telling you so was right.

MsThang: Moving on, the type of men I've been going out with for the last decade are basically all the same man with a different wrapping.

BlackCat: Okay.

MsThang: Maybe if I stop dating the same type, I'll finally find the guy I'm looking for.

BlackCat: So now you're going to go out with ugly, homeless, poor guys?

Bailey gave a very unladylike snort at Cat's reply. She was desperate to get out of her rut but not crazy. Bailey had no intention of changing her standards, just broadening them some.

MsThang: No. Just rework some criteria.

BlackCat: And this is going to rid you of your sexual drought how?

MsThang: Well, the new man plan isn't, but my other plan will.

BlackCat: What plan?

MsThang: I call it my "Bonus Package" plan.

BlackCat: A bonus…for whom?

Bailey was so pleased with her plan she couldn't wait to share the name of her soon-to-be lover with Cat.

MsThang: Sebastian.

BlackCat: Oh Bay, no!

Surprised at her comment, Bailey sat back from the screen. She had expected Cat to try to talk her out of it, but not for her to be aghast at the idea of taking their mutual friend Sebastian Emerzian for a lover.

In fact, the more Bailey thought about taking Sebastian for a lover, the more she liked the idea.

Sebastian wasn't seeing anyone. He wasn't in love with her and next to Cat, he was her best friend. What could possibly be better than making love with a friend?

BlackCat: It's a terrible idea. Sebastian isn't the type of man…for you.

With a smug smile, Bailey quickly typed the one word that proved her entire point.

MsThang: Exactly.

* * * * *

Sebastian sat behind the overlarge mahogany desk like a man born to it. He had a horrendous amount of work before him, the stack of case files proved it and yet he couldn't seem to concentrate. Not a good thing for a lawyer with the responsibility of keeping his corporate clients in business.

When his personal line rang, Sebastian smiled. Not many knew the number so the possibility of it being Bailey on the other end of the line was high.

"Hey, sweetness. Have you decided what you want to watch tonight?"

The utter silence made his cheeks burn with embarrassment. Maybe it wasn't Bailey who'd called after all.

"Uh, he-hello?"

He'd just about decided it was a prank and he'd made a complete ass out of himself when he heard her giggle. "Whooo, that was funny. You know, 'Bastian, I don't think I've ever heard you stutter before."

"Damn brat." Sebastian chuckled into the phone. "So, we still on for tonight?"

"Oh yeah, we're on all right."

Something about her voice sounded different, more provocative and sultry. Sebastian shook his head. He must be hearing things.

"Okay then. I'll pick you up at six."

Sebastian ended the conversation but couldn't quite manage to get the slight change in her voice out of his head. The slight change nagged at him as he finished his work and later as he dressed for their un-date. It was the way he thought about their outings—dates that weren't really dates.

Un-dates.

* * * * *

Instead of sitting across from him as she normally did, Bailey scooted onto the booth's bench seat beside Sebastian until they were so close her scent wrapped around him.

"I really hate sitting with my back to the door."

Knowing her penchant for never backing down from an argument, Sebastian decided to remain silent on the subject. He didn't see any reason to point out she'd never seemed to mind before.

Plastering a smile on his face, Sebastian shifted to make the cut of his pants more comfortable. At five feet ten inches, he was just tall enough he could clearly see down the front of Bailey's blouse.

The view he had of the uppermost swell of her breasts made him want to pant. The way they were lifted—as if in offering—by her bra, which was barely covered by the nearly sheer camisole she wore, damn near had him drooling.

With casualness he didn't feel, Sebastian scooted across the seat until there was enough space between them so he could turn his upper body. His intention was to initiate one of their lively conversations but Bailey's wide-eyed stare and wicked smile took his breath and evidently his ability to string words together as well.

"What's the matter with you tonight, 'Bastian? I'm not going to bite." Her sultry words, full of innuendo, were only compounded by the hand she placed on his leg.

But I might, if you keep it up. The words echoed through Sebastian's mind. His chuckle was strained and husky even to his own ears. Evidently he hadn't moved far enough. It took superhuman effort to remain calm and cool when his cock felt so hot and hard he thought he might explode.

For the life of him, Sebastian couldn't figure out what had gotten into him all of a sudden. Bailey always dressed nice and looked hot, but for some reason tonight she was all decked out for a night of seduction, not their normal dinner-and-a-movie wear, and it bothered him a great deal.

Her skirt fit like a second skin. Its length was decent enough, falling just above her knees, but knowing it left her legs gloriously nude made Sebastian long to run his tongue up the smooth expanse of one until he reached her sweet center before nipping his way down the other.

Her breasts were another matter altogether. High and firm, they were absolutely perfect. Not overly large and yet not so small they wouldn't overflow his cupped palm. Just thinking about the succulent globes made him wonder what color her nipples would be.

Damn! Sebastian ran a hand through his hair in agitation. Why now, after all the time they'd been going out as friends, did Bailey decide to dress to kill and act as though she were going to hop on and give him a spur-of-the-moment lap dance?

About the time Sebastian thought he might go out of his mind, a waitress who promptly and efficiently took their order saved him. Bailey smiled at the woman then looked away, her gaze now lingering over the bad boy making his way across the restaurant. The man was tall and muscle-bound.

His eyes were riveted on Bailey, a carnal smile curving his mouth. Was that why she'd gotten so dressed up? Did Bailey plan to use their night out to her benefit by picking up other men at the same time?

Just the thought of it made Sebastian want to roar in anger. Instead he handed Bailey his napkin, allowing his twisted sense of humor full rein.

"Are you okay? Do you have something in your eye?"

She tilted her head to the side just a bit and gave him a look of confusion. With a straight face, he thrust the napkin in her hand. "You were blinking fast, I thought you had something in your eye." Sebastian batted his lashes while struggling not to smile.

"Ohh! You!" Bailey's laughter broke the awkwardness of the moment. Sebastian couldn't help but join in. Heads swiveled in their direction.

It wasn't long after the same waitress brought their food. They talked of mundane things as they ate and then proceeded to share a huge slice of cake. By the time they were done, Sebastian was afraid they might need to be rolled to his car.

It was one of the things he enjoyed most about Bailey. She enjoyed food just as much as he did. Not one time during their friendship had she munched on a stalk of celery bemoaning the fullness of her ass or the possibility she might get a blemish if she actually ate the candy bar she craved.

Like him, Bailey consumed her meal with gusto, enjoying every bite to pass her lips — her full, luscious, pouty lips, which Sebastian could easily picture wrapped around his cock.

"Shit!"

"What's wrong?"

It wasn't until Bailey voiced the question Sebastian realized he hadn't kept his outburst silent. "I, uh… It's getting too crowded in here. You ready to go?"

"Sure but it's my turn to pay."

"Not a chance."

"'Bastian, you agreed we'd take turns treating or go Dutch."

"I don't recall agreeing to any such thing," Sebastian lied. He knew exactly what Bailey was talking about, but as long as he was the guy and she was the girl, he would pay. End of discussion.

Ignoring the inquisitive arch of her brow, Sebastian motioned to the waitress for their ticket. "If it makes you feel better, I'll let you pay for the movie."

"Liar."

She knew him so well. Which meant she knew there was no way he'd allow her to pay for any part of their night out. Once the bill was taken care of, he led Bailey to his car.

It was going to be a long night.

* * * * *

Timing. Seduction was all about perfect timing. Lowered lights, roaring fireplace, even nature was on her side, giving life to the bittersweet symphony of rain beating against the roof. There was no doubt in Bailey's mind tonight was the perfect night to make love with Sebastian.

After an extremely enjoyable dinner, they decided to forgo a movie and retire back to her place where earlier in the evening she had set up the night for her naughty plans. The low light of a nearby lamp flickered off the taupe-colored walls of her living room. Tonight she would make Sebastian hers and quench the thirst for sex burning deep within her body.

With lowered eyes, she leaned forward demurely and offered her unbeknownst future lover a glass of wine but also an orchestrated view of her cleavage. Plumped and spritzed with her favorite fragrance for his enjoyment.

Sebastian's eyes widened a bit and he gave an uncomfortable cough as he took the offered glass from her hand. "Hmm…thank you." His softly spoken words followed Bailey as she strolled away from him, removing her shoes as she went. Allowing her toes to curl into the clean but otherwise plain brown carpet at her feet, she couldn't help but look over her shoulder.

Making her way back across the room, Bailey tried hard to bite back her smile but she couldn't help it. He was just so cute. Not in the Hollywood celluloid dreamboat way with chiseled features and washboard abs, but with sweet green eyes hidden behind wire-framed glasses giving his angular face a boyish quality. Cute was definitely the word for him.

He was not her normal type, which was why he was perfect for what she needed now.

"Are you enjoying your new job?"

"Eck," Bailey waved away his words, refusing to focus on her job. "I don't want to talk about that now."

"Tinell still giving you a hard time? I can get decked out in my lawyer finery and threaten to sue her if you want."

"Sue her for what?" she smiled. Cute and protective, definitely best friend qualities. Not exactly qualities for a fuck buddy but Bailey was willing to work around it. "It's just a job, 'Bastian. Something to occupy my time for seven and a half hours a day. Nothing more, nothing less."

"It's harassment, Bailey, and you shouldn't have to put up with it."

"Find me a job with a gay boss and I won't."

"Being beautiful is such a hardship, isn't it?"

Bailey rolled her eyes at the amusement in his voice. Sebastian was always teasing her about her looks. His teasing words were the only proof she'd had since their meeting earlier in the year he'd even noticed her looks.

She wasn't vain or anything, but Bailey knew she was attractive. Just as she knew Sebastian thought she was, he'd just never made a move to do anything about it. At first Bailey had been relieved. It had been a really long time since she had a male friend who was just a friend.

Sitting on the plush surface of her multi-colored suede couch, Bailey swung her legs until they lay flat on the couch cushions with her freshly pedicured feet resting on his black slacks. Arching her left foot, she brushed her ankle against his taut stomach, an action that drew his attention down to her crimson-stained toenails.

"Do you like this color?" Raising her leg a bit, she offered him the chance to follow her long brown leg to the apex of her thighs. "I felt the need to pamper myself today. I had a pedicure and a manicure, plus I let them pluck and wax me. I'm as smooth as a baby's bottom. Want to feel?"

"Why do people compare smoothness to baby bottoms? What freak is out there caressing butts and then saying, 'Hey, you know what this feels like?'"

"Sebastian…"

With brows furrowed, he looked at her. "I'm serious. If you think about it, it's a really twisted saying."

"You're twisted."

"You're the one rubbing baby bottoms and then rubbing your legs. Freak."

"I'm a freak?"

"A little, but I'm not here to judge."

He wasn't supposed to be there for comic relief either. Pouting, Bailey pulled back and crossed her arms over her chest. Leave it to Sebastian to make seduction complicated. He was supposed to be bowled over. Pouncing on her with desire, not making lame jokes about baby asses.

"I think we should have sex." The words rushed out of her mouth unfortunately at the same time as Sebastian took a drink.

The wine didn't stay down long though. Instead, it came up in a beautiful red geyser as he choked and spurted, "What!?"

"What" wasn't exactly what she had been going for. Surprise, Bailey had expected. The look of horror, followed by wine shooting out of Sebastian's nose, splattering across the smooth surface of her end table before landing in several little puddles on her carpet, she hadn't been prepared for.

In fact, his astonishment bothered her a bit. Leaning forward, she grabbed a napkin off her artfully decorated-with-seduction-in-mind table and shoved it at him. "You don't have to look so thrilled."

"Thrilled?" He choked, still grasping for air. "What the hell has gotten into you?"

"Nothing." And that was the problem. Bailey was officially approaching her longest sexual drought since she'd first lost her virginity to Andy Hill after her senior high-school prom.

She was horny, frustrated and needed to feel a man's body pressing down on hers. Who better to fill her need than her newly acquired male best friend? Unfortunately, Sebastian didn't actually have the thrilled look she'd been expecting. "What's wrong? Don't you want to have sex with me?"

"Sex? With you? Bailey, were you getting high in the kitchen?"

Offended more for his sake than her own, Bailey sat back with a jerk, the plushness of the oversized pillows at her back all but swallowing her. "You think I need to be high to contemplate having sex with you?"

"You have to be something," Sebastian stood. "We've been hanging out for the last six months or so and this is the first time you've ever hinted at wanting to take our friendship to a different level."

Had it really been so long? Six months was roughly the amount of time it had been since she'd had sex, but surely they had been spending time together a lot longer than that. "So?"

"So, why now?"

"What's wrong with now?"

21

"What's right about now?" he countered, ever the lawyer. "I mean, was it the wine?"

"No, of course not." Bailey stood, not liking the way Sebastian was glaring down at her. "I've been thinking about our relationship. About how much I really like you."

"Like me?"

"Yes, you know I do. We have such a great time together. I'm not seeing anyone, and unless something has changed in the last forty-eight hours, neither are you."

"So you want to see each other?"

"Naked."

"Naked...only?"

"Yes." Finally he understood what she was getting at. "I mean, your friendship is very important to me. Almost as important as Cat's. But I want more, and I think if you think about it, you might too. We can have it all, best friends plus sexual satisfaction. Friends with benefits."

Friends with benefits? Bailey's less-than-attractive term rolled around in Sebastian's head even as he fought to keep his cock at rest. She was a minx of the worst kind. Always testing the patience of the men around her. Although not the spoiled, fit-throwing type, she was a master at getting her way, more persistent than most.

She was trouble with a capital T. Sebastian had known it since the day Mason and Catarena had introduced them all those months ago. Hell, back then he'd actually felt sorry for her boyfriends. And now here she was propositioning him.

"So, you're looking for a no-strings-attached affair?" Sebastian once again took his seat then watched as Bailey made her way back to the couch.

When she sat, he leaned in close, inhaling the intoxicating scent of her perfume as it blended with her arousal. She was in need of sex, of a cock to fill her depths and thought him good enough to fit the bill. How kind of her.

Her big brown eyes lit up. She was evidently happy he finally understood what she was talking about. "Not necessarily. I'm not sure what I'd call a sexual relationship between us but I think affair might be taking it a bit too far."

It was getting harder and harder for Sebastian to hide his irritation. To cover up how badly he wanted to deposit her facedown over his lap and spank some sense into her, he reached a hand out and caressed the soft flesh of her cheek.

The thought of baring the mocha flesh of her ass for the flat of his hand was enough to send every drop of blood flowing through his veins south. Sebastian idly wondered what Bailey would do if she knew of his penchant for spanking, both for erotic pleasure and as a form of punishment.

His love of a woman's nicely rounded ass could be considered a fetish, one not many understood, and yet one he refused to hide from any woman he planned to spend any amount of time with sexually.

"Why don't you explain it to me then?" Sebastian tried to get his mind off her delectable ass and back on the conversation at hand.

Bailey placed her hand on his leg just above his knee, making matters worse. "Well," she said while stroking little circles on his inner thigh with slender fingers. "We would still be friends enjoying each other's company. As an added perk, we'd also have a bit of mutual fun when we needed it."

"So, friends who fuck?"

She looked a bit shocked by his choice of words. Sebastian had always treated her like a lady, including for the most part, watching his language.

Sebastian noticed Bailey didn't let his foul language sway her for long before she nodded, a beautiful wide smile on her face. Damn, she was gorgeous! Gorgeous and about to learn she wouldn't always get what she wanted, at least where he was concerned.

With the ease born of a man used to being in charge, he moved into Bailey's personal space. Sebastian's goal was to leave her breathless, to invade her every sense and leave her body craving his touch and his taste. The key was not to allow himself to get pulled into a trap of his own making.

He turned the hand still stroking her face until her cheek was cupped in his palm. "Come here." Although quietly done, his words were an order, an order that caused Bailey to raise a perfectly arched brow.

The subtle censure aimed toward him reeked of a challenge, one Sebastian would gladly accept. "This was your idea, brat." He lifted his lips in a wicked grin to ease the sting of his words.

Bailey huffed an aggravated breath before moving closer. Sebastian said nothing in return, nor did he change his features to show his triumph. To do so would put an end to not only any possibility of eventually having her bound to his bed with his mark across the full globes of her ass, but it would also more than likely end their friendship as well.

She continued to move until they were pressed together, thigh to thigh, before she turned to him. Her breath smelled of wine, making Sebastian long to taste her. With calmness he didn't feel, he pulled her in for a lingering kiss.

Her taste burst in his mouth, tempting and sweet. Bailey tried to take over, using her tongue to urge him on, but Sebastian was ready for her actions and easily thwarted her efforts.

Not one to give up control, Bailey broke the kiss then got to her feet. She stood before him like the goddess she was. The way her full lips glistened with the blended moisture of their kiss, as well as the subtle taste of her on his tongue, left Sebastian wanting more. Much more.

The slender fingers of her hand wrapped around his then tugged, pulling him to his feet. He stopped her before she towed him down the hallway to her bedroom because once there, he wouldn't be able to stop. It would be a "to hell with it" type of moment where Sebastian would end up tying her to the bed belly down and spanking her while he sank his cock deep within the warm folds of her pussy.

Bailey protested slightly as he pinned her to the wall. When he wedged one of his legs high between her thighs, she stopped. Sebastian took her mouth beneath his, stroking and tasting her with his tongue. She was warm and wet and tasted so damned good Sebastian thought he might come in his pants without her ever even touching him.

And as if the feel of her mouth wasn't enough, the heat of her core pressed against his trouser-clad leg was almost his undoing. Just thinking about how hot she was urged him to deepen the kiss, to insist on more, to take what Bailey might not even imagine offering.

She wiggled against him, riding his leg while searching for a climax Sebastian had no intention of allowing. To slow her frenzied movements, he anchored her head with a hand in her hair. He expected a protest, remembering the warning Catarena had given him so long ago about how Bailey didn't like to have her hair touched, but received nothing but a whimper of need.

It was a sound so unlike anything he expected to hear from the fiercely independent woman in his arms. For a minute Sebastian could do no more than stare into her eyes, trying to extract what she was feeling.

The feel of her hand on his cloth-covered cock quickly brought him out of the lust-induced stupor stealing him of his wits. It was time to up the ante, to show Bailey why he couldn't be her once-in-a-while lover.

Using tongue and teeth, he nipped at her mouth, capturing the fullness of her lower lip between his teeth. He pulled away as much as their positions allowed, causing Bailey to follow. At her gasp, he laved the tiny hurt away.

She wriggled and moaned against him. When she was so restless he feared she'd end up a puddle at his feet, Sebastian used his free hand to lift her skirt, loving the feel of her silky skin against his fingertips. He'd started at the knee, tracing his way up her inner thigh, taking her skirt with him until his fingers rested against the fabric of her barely there panties.

Without thought to his actions, he twisted the thin bikini hip string around his finger and yanked. The sound of rending fabric sounded loud in the otherwise silent room. Bailey gasped and tried to pull away but he had no intention of letting her go.

Her struggles were short-lived, abruptly ending when Sebastian traced her moist folds with his finger. After gathering her cream, he circled her clit. His ever-lessening circles continued to get smaller and smaller until he was right on the edge of her overly sensitive bundle of nerves yet never quite coming in contact.

"Oh! Touch me, 'Bastian, touch me."

Sebastian continued his sensual torture, loving the breathless sound of her words against his mouth.

"I am touching you, sweetness." He wanted to do so much more than touch her. The thought of leaving without tasting her cream or fingering her tight ass nearly brought him to his knees. But he had to remain tough. This wasn't about his pleasure, it was about her punishment.

Sebastian changed the course of his finger, moving until he was knuckle-deep in her wet sheath while kissing his way down the graceful column of her neck where he could feel the thundering of her pulse.

She was magnificent and she was going to be so pissed.

When she was on the verge of orgasming, Sebastian pulled back. He schooled his features into a mask of indifference and waited for the storm to hit.

26

"Wh—" Her confused eyes stared at him as her throat worked to swallow. "Why the hell did you stop?" There was the fire he knew would come.

"Because you needed a taste of what kind of man I am." Sebastian backed away, his eyes fixed on the torn panties still looped around her ankle. Her gaze followed his, her eyes widened a bit in shock, as if she'd forgotten his impatience. "I'm not the kind of man you want for a screw every now and then, Bailey. I don't work that way."

Her eyes flashed and for a second Sebastian thought she might just launch herself at him, claws and all.

"I think it would be best if we stick with friendship and you stick with what you know, pretty boys who play nice."

Then, knowing their relationship would forever be changed, Sebastian leaned in for one last kiss, one last taste of her luscious lips before he turned and walked away.

Chapter Two

ဢ

The red glowing lights of her alarm clock seemed to mock Bailey as it flashed its bright neon radiance in her tired eyes. A lot of good being tired did when she couldn't fall asleep. Whether it was her conscience or her annoyance, Bailey had tossed and turned for the better part of three hours, no closer to sleep than she had been when she'd first lain down.

And it was all his fault.

The traitor. The betrayer. The orgasm Nazi. How dare Sebastian turn her down?

Even in her mind, the words sounded snotty. It wasn't as if Bailey thought he should be grateful because of who she was, more of because of what she was. Which was damn great in bed.

They could have had fun. Dirty, mind-numbing, triple-X fun, but Sebastian had to fuck it up and turn her down. Now neither one of them was getting laid tonight.

With a guttural growl, Bailey rolled over for what had to have been the twentieth time and plopped her fist on her goose-down pillow in frustration. This was supposed to be a night of bliss, a night of unbridled passion. Not a night of unrequited satisfaction.

Her body tingled still with an awareness she couldn't get to go away. The sheets, made from finely spun silk, irritated her sensitive skin. Bailey's body felt unlike her own, but like that of a girl on the brink of womanhood. Even as she willed herself to doze, her mind continuously flashed to visions of Sebastian and his talented fingers.

With a simple touch he had made her body tremble like the San Andreas Fault. Her thighs still quivered from the suppressed passion coursing through her body. She needed to be filled. She needed to be fulfilled. She needed Sebastian.

It was insane.

Dependable, harmless Sebastian was supposed to be…well, safe, for lack of a better word. Not the type of guy who could knock Bailey on her ass. That wasn't what she'd been looking for. Yet he had done it anyway.

The bastard.

Without thought to the consequences, Bailey rolled back over and picked up the phone. Dialing Sebastian's number by heart, she waited impatiently for him to answer. Two a.m. be damned, she wanted answers and she wanted them now.

"'Lo."

The bastard had been asleep. Asleep! While she had been restlessly rolling a new groove in her bed. "Sebastian."

"Bailey, is that you?" His voice sounded a bit more alert but not enough to appease Bailey's anger or frustration.

"How can you sleep at a time like this?"

"Very easily. I lie down, close my eyes and let my mind drift. I've been doing it for years. Surprisingly, it happens around the same time every night."

Bailey refused to be swayed by his dry humor. "What you did tonight was incredibly mean."

"And what you did was incredibly…Bailey."

With a gasp, Bailey sat straight in her bed. "Bastard!"

"Brat."

"You…you…"

"Bastard," he dryly offered. "I think you mentioned that already."

"If you didn't want to have sex, all you had to do was say no. It was just an idea, a very good one, by the way. Nothing to get vindictive over."

"I wasn't being vindictive, Bailey."

"Ha!" Bailey didn't believe him for a second. He was evil. He was mean-spirited. He was the best kisser she'd ever had the misfortune to kiss.

The way he quickly took over the situation had stunned and overwhelmed Bailey. Her body had never been taken to such heights before, just to be let down at the precipice of her climax.

No matter how skillfully she had strummed her aching bud after he'd left, Bailey hadn't been able to quench the fire Sebastian had started inside of her. To be honest, it was what had truly upset her. In less than a few moments, Sebastian had masterfully done what so few men had accomplished before. He had turned the tables on Bailey. Made her crave his touch. Made her crave the man himself.

For that alone Bailey was upset. "If it wasn't vindictiveness, then what was it?"

"You're too used to getting your way, to men falling at your feet whenever you bat your pretty lashes their way. I'm not that man."

"I thought you were my friend."

"Friends don't fuck, Bailey, especially the way I do."

His words aroused her mind. "You think you do it differently than anyone else? I hate to break it to you, 'Bastian, you didn't break the mold when it comes to great sex."

"And that's what's bugging you, isn't it, Bay? You'll never know."

Bailey's finger clicked the phone off the second his words penetrated her oversexed brain. That bastard! As if he were God's gift or something. Tossing the covers to the side, she rose from her bed angrier than when she had lain down three and a half hours ago.

She was going to kill him. No, death was too good for the asshole. Instead, she was going to tie him up, torture him and then kill him. Wait, scratch the tying up part. The dirty little freak might enjoy it.

The phone wailed out in the middle of her rant, stopping Bailey in her tracks. With narrowed eyes, she stalked back to the bed, intent on giving Sebastian a piece of her mind.

"You bas…"

Before she could get the swear out, Sebastian roared, "Don't you ever hang up on me or I'll tan your ass so quickly you won't be able to sit down for weeks."

Bailey gasped at his brazen audacity. "Try it and I'll rip you a new asshole."

"Is that a challenge?" The heat in his voice did little to quench the fire smoldering inside of her.

Bailey couldn't resist firing back. "Do you want to try me?"

"More than you'll ever know, but as I stated, you can't handle me."

The dare in his tone was more than Bailey could take. It was one thing to finger her and leave her panting after him like a brazen whore, but it was quite another for him to insinuate she couldn't match him sexually. Topping men in bed was one of the things Bailey did best. Even on a bad day, she could fuck him into a coma. "I can handle anything you can dish out. If you recall, it wasn't me who put a halt on this evening's festivities."

"I did you a favor. I'm not one to share, Bailey, or one to back down. You should tread lightly with me and be thankful I let you go with just a warning."

"Consider me warned but not afraid."

"You should be, little girl."

Before Bailey could get in another word, Sebastian hung up the phone. Torn between intrigue and irritation, Bailey slammed her cordless phone back down into the charger.

Fucking men.

* * * * *

It had been nearly a week. A goddamned motherfucking week since he'd heard a word from Bailey. Hell, he'd probably scared her for good, ranting and raving about whipping her ass but, dammit! She'd pushed.

Part of him wanted with everything in his being to call her and make it all better. But the other half of him knew better. If Bailey wanted to have a relationship that went past friendship, she would have to be told about his darker side and learn to embrace his kinks.

On that account, Sebastian wasn't willing to compromise. As a young man, he'd tried on more than one occasion to hide his fetish and to have what others considered a normal sex life. What a fucking fiasco it had turned out to be.

Sweat dripped from his forehead and into his eyes as he dribbled the ball from one end of the court to the other, but Sebastian wouldn't relent. He'd come to the conclusion the only way to keep Bailey off his mind was to stay busy.

"What gives?" Mason asked the question at the same time he stole the ball.

"She's driving me insane." Exasperation was evident in Sebastian's voice.

Mason sunk a two-pointer, winning the game before turning to Sebastian. "By 'she' I assume you mean Bailey."

Sucking air into his lungs, Sebastian bent at the waist and rested his hands on his knees. He nodded his head in answer to Mason's question. "She's something else," he added when he could finally breathe again.

"Sounds as if things are getting serious."

"That's the problem, the brat's not serious. She's looking for a fuck and figured I'd be safe. I turned her down and she hasn't spoken to me since."

The look on Mason's face was comical. "You mean to tell me the two of you have been going out as friends? Only friends...for six months!" He seemed absolutely appalled by the idea.

"I enjoy her company."

"But you want to fuck her too."

Sebastian didn't like the way those words sounded. She might be a brat and looking for a sex-only relationship but he wouldn't allow anyone, not even Mason, to talk about her. Bailey was a lady. "Don't go there."

Mason lifted his hands in mock surrender. "Oh hell, my friend. You are so far gone you'll never get back. I almost feel sorry for you."

Rubbing the back of his neck did nothing to ease the tension tying his body in knots. "Yeah, she kind of blindsided me the other night. I had been doing so well keeping her in the 'friends only' compartment of my brain, but the minute she aimed her sultry smile at me and invited me to her bed, she shot my plan all to hell.

"Now I have no idea where we stand. Every time I think about what I want to do to her delectable ass, I cringe, thinking about her reaction. How in the hell do you explain to a woman you plan to make more than just a one-night stand that in order to get your rocks off, you have to spank her?"

Sebastian shook his head. Just thinking about the conversation, with Bailey on the listening end, made him fear for his wellbeing.

"Then don't tell her. Show her."

The thought of just showing her as Mason so easily suggested made him laugh. "Oh yeah, I could see her just sitting idly by watching me play with another woman. Something about the brat makes me think she'd just as soon castrate me."

Mason winced at his choice of words. "It doesn't have to be you she watches, Sebastian. Think about it."

"I'm all thought out. If you've got a plan that might put me out of my misery, spill it."

Mason dribbled the basketball a few times before once again giving Sebastian his full attention. He seemed to be weighing a decision. "Catarena invited Bailey to The Boulevard Saturday night."

"Fuck that! It isn't going to happen." Sebastian shook his head in denial. Something in the back of his mind warned him he had no say at all in what Bailey chose to do, but another part of him, the part that wanted to dominate her, reared its head and fought for supremacy.

"I had pretty much the same reaction."

"I bet Catarena was thrilled." Sebastian couldn't help the smart-ass remark.

"Yeah, well...let's just say the argument made the evening an interesting one. Needless to say, I agreed to the outing on the condition I tag along."

Sebastian should have known there was a catch. Even though The Boulevard had recently changed hands and was now owned by a friend who ran in the same circle with Mason and Sebastian, it was still a fetish club. There was no way Mason would have agreed to the outing without attending.

"I think I might just have to crash your little party." Bailey was going to be beyond angry. She was going to be downright irate, but at least Sebastian would be able to show her a taste of what he needed when it came to his sexual preferences. He couldn't help but heave a sigh of relief knowing soon things would be settled.

Plans immediately started filtering their way through Sebastian's mind. He would have to call Natalie Griffith, The Boulevard's new owner. He wanted to be sure a spanking scene was set up for the night, preferably in a private room with only Catarena and Mason in attendance with them.

"From the look on your face, I'd say it's a good idea." Mason grabbed a towel to wipe the sweat from his brow. He made his way across the court before turning. "See you Saturday."

Sebastian could hardly wait, but wait he would. It seemed as if the days crawled by at a snail's pace. By the time Saturday finally rolled around, he would need to see a doctor about the ulcer he had surely developed.

Everything was set up. The only thing left for Sebastian to do was to crash the party and make it past Bailey's defenses. He was sure facing a pack of rabid wolves would be easier.

* * * * *

Music blared from hidden speakers but other than loud music, the place didn't resemble the dark dungeon it once had. New paint covered the walls and for those who weren't into dancing there were cozy conversation areas set up in out-of-the-way alcoves. The hallway leading to the back rooms was now painted a high-gloss red. It no longer brought forth feelings of unease, as if the person entering were walking straight to their doom.

Sebastian spotted Bailey the minute his eyes adjusted to the dim lighting. She sat at a small table with Catarena and Mason, right where Mason said they would be.

It was obvious when Bailey noticed him as well because she shot a look of pure malice in Mason's direction.

Sebastian made it to the table just in time to hear Bailey's hissed words. "I should have known. Million Dollar Mason doesn't know how to play fair."

"Bailey!" Catarena, who knew Mason and his limits, was obviously worried about her friend's outburst.

Sebastian took the vacant seat next to Bailey and watched Mason, who merely arched a brow. "Keep it up, brat, and I'll warm your ass long before Sebastian gets the chance."

Sebastian didn't like the sound of that but he was enjoying the byplay. There was something about Bailey's sassiness that made his cock rock-hard in a matter of seconds. If she would come around to his way of thinking, at least where sex was concerned, they could have a hell of a good time.

Sebastian's palm tingled just thinking about it.

* * * * *

It would be a lie of the highest order for Bailey to say Sebastian's presence there tonight was a surprise. In all truth, not only had she been expecting him, she had hoped he would come.

Of course, it would do no good for him to know. If he did, it probably wouldn't take him much longer to realize how much she'd missed him over the past week. Bailey didn't know when it happened or why, but her days didn't feel as complete when she didn't have him to talk to.

Before the argument, their late night phone calls had become a big part of their nightly routine. Sometimes it would be to laugh over a horrible date one of them had, sometimes it was just to catch up on each other's day. But as quickly as the images of their phone calls came to mind, bringing with them a smile Bailey couldn't resist, so did the quick flash of anger when she recalled their last phone call.

Thinking about that night was all Bailey needed in order to get her mental shields in place. Ignoring Mason's spanking comment because of the ick factor and ignoring Sebastian for his dick factor, a la finger-a-girl-against-a-wall-then-don't-allow-her-to-get-off reason, she turned her attention to Catarena, who was looking somewhat peeved herself.

It was good to know her girl had her back. "For this to be a girls' night out, there sure seems to be an abundance of dick here tonight."

"Or maybe just two dicks too many," Catarena agreed, glaring at Mason, who turned narrowed eyes from Bailey to Catarena.

"You knew I was coming," he reminded her with a sneer.

"I know you badgered your way into coming." Catarena crossed her arms over her chest and turned toward Mason, as if readying herself for a fight.

"See what you started," Sebastian teased in a mock whisper to Bailey.

Rolling her eyes, Bailey pushed back her chair and stood. Catarena and Mason's bickering was something the duo did best and often. Their power struggle had nothing to do with Bailey—with them it was just another form of foreplay. Bailey had witnessed it often enough to know now was the perfect time for her to make an escape. She doubted if her presence or lack thereof would even be noticed once they got started.

But she forgot about Sebastian. "Where are you going?"

His question didn't stop Bailey in her tracks. His hand around her wrist did though. The simple touch caused Bailey to catch her breath as her heart shimmied a bit inside her chest.

What the heck was going on?

They had touched thousands and thousands of times. But never before had his touch seem to singe through her skin as it traveled up her arm, down her chest and lower, to tease the lips covering her sex. It was a simple touch on her wrist. Yet, she was wet with just the thought of what more they could be doing. What more they had been doing.

Stop it, Bay. Get yourself together now.

With what she hoped was an arrogant glare, Bailey looked at his hand and back at him. Instead of irritating him as she hoped, Sebastian seemed to find her disdain amusing.

He even had the nerve to raise a brow. "Well...?"

"The restroom...Master."

"Master?"

"Considering our surroundings, I thought it fitting." Pulling her hand away from him, Bailey resisted the urge to rub her tingling wrist. She walked away from the table with her head held high and an extra wiggle in her hips. Without a doubt, Bailey knew Sebastian was watching her walk away, she could practically feel his intense stare follow her all the way across the crowded room.

He was going to wait for her. Bailey knew it as surely as she knew the redhead sharing the bathroom mirror with her had fake boobs. Nice fake boobs, but those babies were fake.

I wonder who her doctor is? Looking at her own small breasts, Bailey wondered if he would work on a payment plan.

Chuckling at the thought, Bailey lifted her gaze from her breasts and stared at the rest of her. She was looking good tonight. Maybe not fetish club good, but definitely "see what you're missing" good. And if everything went right, he would.

Then the real fun could begin.

So she had blown the first girl rule by letting Sebastian know he could have her. Unfortunately for her though, he didn't want her...or didn't want her in such a way, which really confused her to hell and back.

He wanted her. That much Bailey knew. She just didn't get the connection with the how he wanted her.

After adding just a dollop more of gloss to her full bottom lip, Bailey adjusted the girls so they appeared full and plump and readied herself for their next encounter. As she stepped out of the bathroom, Bailey was unpleasantly surprised to see he wasn't there. Surprise flickered across her face as she stepped farther into black leather garnished walls, which flanked the sleek waiting area, and looked around with disbelief.

He hadn't come. She'd waited, primped and talked to herself for nothing.

Angry now, Bailey pushed through the leather swinging doors, intent on giving Sebastian a piece of her mind, when a low, deep chuckle rose from behind her.

Turning quickly, Bailey spotted him leaning against the red velvet walls of the outer room. His stance gave off a sense of confidence many men couldn't pull off sincerely. Yet Sebastian was sincere. He was one of the cockiest, most honest men Bailey had ever met. His outlook on life was one of the many things that had drawn him to her in the first place. It was as if she were looking in a mirror.

His dark button-up shirt and black slacks looked positively sinful against all of the red. Sinful and inviting all at the same time. The cocky grin meant only one thing. He knew she'd expected him to be waiting on the other side.

"What?" Bailey tried to walk past him but Sebastian wasn't having it.

Grabbing her arm, he spun her around until she was leaning against the wall.

"You know what."

She eyed him as he leaned in closer. With her back against the wall, Bailey was at his mercy. Unable to move one way or the other unless he permitted—not that she was in any huge hurry to move. Because they were so close in height, Sebastian didn't tower over her and it made the way he leaned into her even more intimate.

Butterflies on speed were fluttering around in her stomach. Bailey wanted to pretend to be cool, hell it was her trademark, but she was having a difficult time just remembering how to speak.

When Sebastian reached his hand out to caress her cheek, Bailey moved her face slightly and found her voice. "This reeks of familiarity. This time though, could you not rip my panties? I'm actually quite fond of these."

His chuckle brushed across her ear as he leaned in closer. "Still irritated at me, I see."

"I'm not irritated." The words came out a bit hesitant. She was having a hard time pouting when he was so close to her, smelling so damn good. Sebastian needed to back up so she could gather her wits, but she refused to be the one to ask him. It would be like admitting defeat.

"Then why haven't you called me?"

His words caught her attention. Turning her head until they were eye to eye, Bailey threw the question back at him. "Why haven't you called me?"

"You're so cute."

"Puppies are cute," she fumed.

"You're no puppy." Tilting his head to the side, he continued as if in afterthought, "Although you do occasionally act like a bit—"

Bailey dug her nails into the solid muscle of his chest and warned, "Say it and it will be you lying on the floor."

"Testy." Sebastian grinned as he pushed into her hands.

"You're liking this, aren't you?" Bailey tightened her grip into him as she watched his eyes dilate.

Sebastian brought his hand between them and brushed ever so slightly against her pebbled nipples protruding from her dress. "So are you."

"Is this your thing, 'Bastian?" Her voice was hoarse now but her grip was still firm. "A little pain?"

"I enjoy a lot of things, Bay. The question is, are you willing to find out what you like?"

Sebastian watched a jumble of emotions chase their way across Bailey's face. She was a hard case to crack, a woman used to being in control and not showing what she felt.

It was a good thing he'd been observant, because in the short time they'd been close, Sebastian had managed to learn a whole lot about Bailey. Like the fact she felt the need to be in control. She also had a tendency to make sarcastic comebacks when nervous and unsure of herself. It was a shield she wielded to keep from getting hurt.

The bite of her fingernails as they dug into his chest only intensified the arousal coursing through his veins, pushing him closer to the edge. Not wanting to take the chance of losing control, Sebastian grasped Bailey's wrists and forced the palms of her hands down his chest.

When Sebastian felt her fingers on his belt, he thought his knees would buckle. Instead, in a movement so fast Bailey didn't have time to struggle, he gently twisted one hand to the small of her back, arching her body against him in the process.

Her brown eyes were wide with shock and arousal. Her breath quickened, causing her chest to rapidly rise and fall. The choppy motion did all sorts of wonderful things to her breasts.

Sebastian leaned into her, his breath fanning against the pulse point where neck and shoulder met. Bailey struggled a bit when he laved her with the tip of his tongue. She tasted sweet and tangy.

"Settle down, sweetheart." He kept his voice low and calm, far from the way he truly felt.

A nearly silent sigh burst from her lips when he suckled her neck. Sebastian couldn't help but smile at the unusual sound of submission coming from his brat's lips. When she snuggled against him, nearly climbing his body, Sebastian growled low in his throat.

Bailey flexed her hands against his hold but Sebastian had no intention of letting go. Still holding the one hand firmly behind her back, he pressed the other lower until the warmth of her palm covered his ever-growing erection.

"Does this answer your question, Bay? Does the feel of my cock ready to explode against your hand tell you exactly what you do to me?"

She jerked back as if someone had just doused her with a bucket of cold water. The look on her face warned Sebastian she wasn't going to give in easily. Bailey was going to fight the unknown until he forced her to see exactly what it was she was missing.

"What are you doing to me?"

"I'm not doing anything you don't want, Bailey. You came out of the ladies' room looking for me." Sebastian held up a hand when she opened her mouth to protest. "You and I both know it, so don't make a liar out of yourself by denying it."

She was angry and confused, a combination that could fuck everything up in no time. Sebastian moved them back into the main area of the club, noticing Catarena and Mason were just leaving the table, heading toward the section of the club where private rooms were set up for scene play.

"Come on, Bay. I think it's time you see exactly what it is I like. You need to know just what you'll be getting yourself into if we take this any further."

Sebastian casually motioned toward where Catarena and Mason were winding their way through the crowd. Bailey seemed wary and a bit unsure, but the way her nipples peaked against the thin fabric of her top told a different story.

She might be unsure but she was also curious. Together, it was a combination Sebastian was more than ready to deal with.

* * * * *

It was extremely hard for him to remember Bailey wasn't used to the scene. She wasn't used to seeing people in relationships out of the norm and although he wasn't into BDSM per se, Sebastian did enjoy some of the lifestyle's finer points.

His love for the sweet curve of a woman's ass, as well as turning it dusky from the palm of his hand or whatever implement he decided to use, might be the kink he enjoyed best, but add to it a bit of bondage and he was in heaven. Those two things were the reason he'd requested the scene room be set up as it was.

Behind the closed door of the room was a platform, which would act as a stage. On it was a four-poster bed. The navy blue coverlet shimmered in the dim light, looking like the sea at night. Very soothing.

On the far side of the room, front and center of the platform, sat two couches. Catarena and Mason were already comfortably ensconced on the plush surface of one. Sebastian led Bailey across the room to the other.

They had just sat when the curtain behind the platform opened slightly and out walked a man and a woman. The two were nearly equal in height but that was where all similarities stopped. The man was lean and athletic while the woman had generous curves. Sebastian smiled. He'd asked for the best and since Natalie knew what she was doing, he had to assume these two were it.

The lights were dim but not so low the couple couldn't be clearly seen as they began caressing each other. When he felt Bailey stiffen beside him, Sebastian placed a hand firmly on her thigh.

"Relax."

Sebastian watched her gaze dart around the room. When she focused back on the platform, it was almost comical the way her jaw dropped, but instead of jumping out of her seat as he expected, she clenched her thighs together and squirmed. Before them on the platform the woman was now bound to the headboard, belly down. Pillows beneath her hips raised her ass in the air perfectly.

In the man's hand was a flogger, one Sebastian had seen on many occasions. In many ways it was more of a novelty but it served the purpose. The heart cutouts on the flogger's leather surface would leave nice pink hearts on the flesh of the recipient without inflicting more than a sting. Sebastian would have to thank Natalie for thinking of the added touch.

This time, Bailey was the one who did the touching. Her hand settled on his thigh. And then, as if unaware of what she was doing, she squeezed. Was she afraid for the woman who was obviously moaning in ecstasy? Sebastian doubted it, but wasn't willing to chance being wrong.

"Bay?"

"Hmmm?" Her eyes were riveted on the platform. Sebastian knew the feeling. Even after all the women he'd flogged over the years, in both punishment and for the sheer pleasure of it, he'd never gotten used to the intensity of seeing it done to someone else.

The woman was now writhing on the bed, whimpering in need as her master relentlessly fingered her. When the man raised the hand holding the flogger high in the air, Bailey's eyes went as wide as saucers. The sound of the first blow landing caused her to jump. Only Sebastian settling his mouth over hers smothered the startled yelp she'd not been able to hold back.

The sound of leather against flesh rang throughout the room, as did the labored breathing of both the man and woman occupying the bed on the stage, one giving the intense combination of pleasure and pain and the other receiving.

"Okay?" Sebastian asked when he finally ended the kiss.

Bailey, who'd kept her eyes open during their kiss, continued to watch closely. "I'm fine. She's the one I'm worried about."

Sebastian choked back a laugh. God, she was more woman than he deserved. Instead of running scared, she sat there riveted to the spot, all but squirming in her seat, and was still able to crack jokes.

"Listen to her, Bay. Listen close and you'll know she's fine." Bailey leaned forward, her hand still on his thigh, and listened, just as he'd instructed.

"Oh God! Please…please fuck me. Please." The bound woman seemed to be chanting the words between gasps and moans. When she turned her face so those watching could clearly see, it was obvious she was enjoying every minute of her erotic punishment.

Sebastian pulled Bailey back against him. With a finger on her cheek, he turned her face. After placing a tender kiss on her lips, he asked, "So what do you think?"

She cocked her head in that magnificent way of hers before a wicked gleam settled in her eye. "I'm not sure about all this spanking shit, but I think she's got the 'Oh God…fuck me' part right."

Chapter Three

ഇ

Who would have ever thought it? It was actually possible to be aroused and utterly confused all at the same time. Part of Bailey wanted to shield her eyes and bury her head under a pillow to block out all the moans and groans. But the baser part of her couldn't tear her gaze away.

She was spellbound.

The bound woman quivered as if in ecstasy. With every strike of the whipping thingy, Bailey felt a tug deep in her groin. Her muscles tensed as the leather hearts rose back in the air before settling down with a resounding swat on the whimpering woman's backside.

This was unreal.

Out of the corner of her eye, she could see Sebastian watching her. His gaze seemed glued to her face, as if waiting for her to say something. He was in for a world of disappointment though, because her ability to speak was long gone. All she could do was stare and ache.

Bailey could feel her fingers tightening on Sebastian's leg but she felt as if it was beyond her power to stop them. Her body craved something she never dared to dream of before, but Bailey didn't know how to deal with it.

From the corner of the room, Bailey heard a moan of satisfaction, which broke her gaze from the show center stage. It was a sound Bailey had heard many nights when Cat and she were roommates and Mason had stayed over. Mason had never been a quiet lover. Tonight didn't seem to be any different.

Expecting to see them locked in an embrace or at the most involved in some light petting, Bailey almost swallowed her tongue when she caught sight of what they were really doing. Somewhere along the line, Cat had dropped to her knees in front of Mason and taken his cock into her mouth.

Mason's eyes were closed in pleasure as he rocked his cock into Cat's hungry mouth. Her hair was pulled back to the side, giving Bailey a perfect angle to watch her pleasure him. Neither of them appeared to notice they had attracted an avid watcher, but then again, it didn't seem as if they cared.

Bailey couldn't help the small gasp to leave her lips any more than she could help staring. A kaleidoscope of contradictions passed through her mind. She shouldn't be watching, hell she shouldn't be aroused, but she was.

Sebastian's deep-throated chuckle caused heat to blossom in her cheeks. Quickly turning her gaze from the couple, Bailey looked back toward the stage with head held high.

"Is this your thing, Bay?" Sebastian leaned in until his mouth brushed the lobe of her ear. "You enjoy watching?"

"Shut up." Her face felt as if it were aflame. It was one thing to be aroused and a complete other for Sebastian to know it.

"I don't think so." To Bailey's surprise, Sebastian reached over, swooped her off the couch and sat her firmly on his lap. With arms as strong as steel he pulled her into him until her back was pressed flush with his chest. Surprisingly it wasn't a bad feeling. Quite the opposite in fact.

His arms felt right wrapped around her, and from the protruding bulge pressing beneath her, Bailey could safely assume she wasn't the only person enjoying the show.

Hallelujah, he was human after all. A very well-endowed human from the feel of it.

"Say it, Bay, tell me you like to watch."

"No." Her words were a whimpering contrast to the small gyrations she was making in his lap. Her body seemed to have a mind of its own and Sebastian's cock was heavy on its priority list.

Bailey struggled halfheartedly in his arms. But really, whom was she fooling? Everything about tonight was turning her on. The show, Cat and Mason, and Sebastian, who was slowly moving his hands down her thighs. Her nipples were rigid peaks begging to be touched and her pussy, wet and throbbing in anticipation, begged for release.

With a slowness that had to be a deliberate tease, Sebastian eased her skirt up as he widened his legs beneath hers, spreading her thighs in the process.

"Sebastian…" His name was a murmur on her lips. The words had barely slipped out before his hands found the damning evidence of her desire, the soaked crotch of her thongs.

When Sebastian growled low in his throat from satisfaction at his discovery and pressed his hard cock against her, Bailey nearly came.

"You like it, don't you, brat? The sound of the flogger marking her, the sight of Mason buried deep in Catarena's throat, is making your little…box…hot." Sebastian punctuated the last words with soft taps on her aching, damp, cloth-covered bud.

"Shut up and—"

Ripping her thongs to the side, he thrust his hard fingers right into her slick passage. "And what, Bay…and what?"

She needed to feel his cock. She needed to ride his hand until she came into a million pieces. She needed him. "Shut up and fuck me."

Grabbing at his pumping hands, Bailey forced him to release her and dropped to her knees in front of him. "Is this what you want, me on my knees in front of you? Is this how you like to play your games?"

Sebastian brought his damp fingers to his mouth. His tongue slid out and lapped at her juices, all the while Bailey watched him in awe. "My kink isn't you on your knees pleasuring me, but it will do for now."

He stood as Bailey remained passive at his feet. Whatever his game was, she wanted to play. If it meant he would be inside of her pumping away, then at this very moment, Bailey was down for whatever.

Passive, safe, dependable Sebastian was nowhere to be seen. He stood before her now like a sovereign. Ready to claim his throne. As he watched her, Sebastian began to unbutton his shirt slowly. Revealing the smooth, rippled flesh of his chest, which was defined but not bulging. He was lean cut, but built very nice all the same. After he dropped the shirt on the couch behind him, he turned to the performers on the bed. "Thank you for the show. You may leave now."

Sebastian slowly walked back to Bailey, desire pouring from his eyes. There would be nothing stopping them now. "Take my cock out, Bailey."

Bailey moved forward a bit so she would be able to block out much of what Mason and Cat were doing but Sebastian stopped her. "No. I want them to watch us just as we watched them."

Jesus, his words alone were about to make her cum. No one spoke of these things. No one did these things, and yet here they were about to perform for each other and Bailey wouldn't have it any other way.

Sebastian sat, positioning himself on the couch so Bailey could see Catarena and Mason as she sucked his cock. The feel of her warm, wet tongue against the heated skin of his aroused shaft was magical. It was damn near as good as he pictured administering her first real spanking would be.

When Bailey ran her thumb over the sensitive head of his cock, collecting the fluid there before bringing it to her lips where her tongue peeked out to lap at it, Sebastian tightened his hand against the back of her head.

"Enough teasing, Bay. Suck me." Sebastian urged her forward with a hand at the back of her head.

"It's your game, babe."

Sebastian wanted to warn her again. He wasn't playing games, but the feel of her lips encircling his cock made coherent thoughts nearly impossible. It was hard to stay in control when bliss and a mind-blowing orgasm were so close.

Concentrating fully on the sensations running through his body kept Sebastian's climax just out of reach. Exactly what he wanted. The control it took to hold off his release only upped the intensity he would feel when he finally allowed himself to come. Sebastian planned to drag Bailey along for the roller-coaster ride as well.

The sound of movement across the room drew Sebastian's attention. He opened his eyes to see Mason positioning Catarena on her knees on the couch. When he cozied up behind her, pushing her forward with a hand on her back until the side of her face and upper body rested on the cushions, Sebastian groaned.

Watching them was arousing but it was the reaction he would see and feel in Bailey as she also watched he was ultimately waiting for.

Mason murmured words to Catarena, words too low for Sebastian to hear, before positioning himself to take her. When Mason's gaze landed on him, Sebastian shook his head. A gentle caress to Bailey's cheek brought her eyes to his.

Her cheeks hollowed around his cock before she released him. Sebastian missed her warmth immediately. Like all men, he enjoyed oral sex but something about having Bailey's lips work his cock gave the sexual act new meaning and depth.

Sebastian pulled Bailey to her feet. "Turn around." His voice was low yet commanding. When she merely stood there, staring at him, he lightly swatted the fleshy curve of her ass. Her eyes widened then narrowed before she spun on her heel.

The sound of her indrawn breath warned she'd caught sight of what was going on across the room. Would she balk at his next command? There was only one way to find out.

"Lift your skirt, baby. Lift it then sit on my lap, on my cock." He loved talking dirty to her just as much as he knew he would. He said the words loud enough to be heard by Catarena and Mason, knowing full well they'd both get off by hearing.

Bailey looked over her shoulder then back to the other side of the room. "Let me know now if this isn't something you can follow through with, Bay. If that's the case, I'll take you home. If not, then I expect you to do as I say."

Her beautiful eyes shot daggers at him but she didn't utter a word.

"If you're staying, do as he says, Bailey, because every time you make him wait, I'm going to spank Catarena." Mason's voice drifted across the room and there was no denying he meant every word he spoke.

Bailey stood as still as a statue. It wasn't until Mason's hand whipped toward Catarena's ass, landing with a crack, which caused her to yelp, that Bailey moved.

She slowly started to raise her skirt. Sebastian's eyes devoured every inch her movements exposed. When she had her skirt bunched around her hips, he was left with an eye-level view of her luscious ass. It was bare. The only covering at all was a thin piece of blue fabric tucked between her cheeks.

"Damn, baby! You have one fine ass. Now, stay just the way you are."

When Bailey turned slightly to look at him, Mason swatted Catarena again, this time making her moan. "It might take a while but eventually it'll click," Mason purred, his gaze locked on Bailey as he rubbed his hand up and down Catarena's back.

"Bastard." Bailey might ache for the release he could give her but Sebastian knew she was nobody's doormat. He smiled then choked on a chuckle when Mason egged her on.

"Mmm, you think?" Mason's cock was fisted in his hand and he was teasing Catarena mercilessly by barely penetrating her before pulling completely out again.

"Fuck, Bay! Would you sit on him already." Catarena's words made Bailey's eyes go wide. A blush stole over her neck and face. She looked absolutely beautiful.

Sebastian pulled Bailey's thong panties over her hips and down her legs. When she stepped out of them, he positioned her where he wanted her and with his hands on her hips, he guided her.

Her round ass against his raging erection nearly unmanned him. "Lean forward."

Her thighs flexed when she did as he asked. Sebastian traced his finger across her slick entrance, ensuring she was as turned on as she looked, before sheathing himself for their protection.

She was so hot and wet he was surprised her cream wasn't sliding down her thighs. Sebastian introduced first one finger and then another into the ultra-tight sheath of her pussy before teasing the tight ring of her anus with his thumb.

Her breath hitched and every muscle in her body tensed in reaction. "Not tonight, not with company to watch, but one night, Bay, one night I'll take you here." Sebastian added the slightest bit of pressure, just enough to tease. "Your ass will grasp my cock so tight, I'll probably come before I get every inch inside of you."

She shivered against him, the muscles of her pussy milking his fingers in tiny trembling waves. "Like that idea, do you? What I forgot to tell you though was before I fuck your beautiful ass, I'm going to spank it until it glows red. I haven't figured out yet whether I'll use my hand or a flogger as you saw tonight, but it will happen."

Bailey bucked against him, wedging his fingers deeper into her channel and the tip of his thumb into her ass. She rocked back and forth, looking for release, unable to stop the need coursing through her body. Sebastian didn't stop fingering her until he felt her inner muscles begin to quiver. When it happened, he pulled his fingers from her and waited.

"Noooo." Her mournful wail nearly made him abandon his plan to make her wait until her need matched his own.

"Not yet, sweetheart. Not until I tell you."

There was a deep growl from across the room and Sebastian knew Mason was tired of waiting to follow through with their pre-thought-out plan.

"Watch them. Watch Mason as he sinks into Catarena and feel as I do the same to you."

Sebastian nudged the head of his cock against her tight opening. Without preamble, he grasped her by the hips and pulled her fully onto him, impaling her with his shaft, filling her, stretching her, in one movement.

"Oh God!"

Reaching around, Sebastian splayed his fingers over where their bodies were connected, feeling how tightly stretched she was around the root of his shaft. It was nearly impossible to stay still but he did so for her benefit. Fingering the sensitive bud of her clit had the desired effect, bringing Bailey even closer to the edge. She wiggled against him, searching for what she needed, insisting with her body he give her the climax she probably wanted more than her next breath.

"Open your legs wider, Bay. Place them over the top of mine." The position would leave her completely open and utterly under his control. With her legs dangling over his, she would have no leverage.

It was a fact she evidently understood because she hesitated, earning Catarena another stinging swat.

"Fuck," she swore even as she positioned her legs over his.

He gave a subtle nod to Mason, who picked up his pace, shafting Catarena with mind-numbing intensity as Sebastian surged into Bailey over and over again.

He rolled and pinched her nipples with one hand while trapping her clit between the fingers of the other, creating sensations her body could no longer deny.

"Come for me, sweetheart. Come for me."

And she did, mewling her pleasure before screaming his name. The sound of her voice mingled with Catarena's in the otherwise quiet room. When she collapsed back on him, Sebastian prayed he hadn't pushed too hard too fast.

* * * * *

Things were moving way too fast too soon. Sex with Sebastian should have been freeing, relieving if nothing else, and yet Bailey felt more confused than when he had turned her down the first time. What the hell had she gotten herself into and why the hell couldn't she forget the way he felt inside of her?

To say sex with him was good would be the understatement of the millennium. Not even in her kinkiest of fantasies had she imagined she could be so free. So willing to be taken and watch others be taken in such a depraved fashion. Everything about the night had aroused and excited her. Including the spanking, which was the most confusing thing of all.

Bailey hadn't been raised to allow a man to hit her. It went against every feminist belief she had and yet she couldn't stop thinking about Sebastian doing what he had whispered to her.

Either Sebastian was completely out of her league or she'd been a very sheltered bird. Bailey had been around the block too many times to believe the latter so it had to be all his fault.

She had gotten what she thought she wanted, which was laid. So now she was fucked, literally and figuratively. Bailey had to put things back in order. A fuck buddy shouldn't be occupying all of her thoughts. It went against the very fiber of the fuck-buddy regulations.

Sebastian wasn't playing by the rules. That bastard!

Now three days later she was avoiding his calls and camped out on the door of her best friend's house, waiting for Cat to come home. Another person she'd been evading until today. Bailey knew she couldn't put it off forever, so after work, she drove over to Cat's house, but of course now that she was ready to talk, Cat was nowhere to be found.

Didn't it just figure?

Maybe Cat didn't want to speak to her either. She did call Bailey the day after the dirty incident, as Bailey had now dubbed it in her brain, and left a message for Bailey to call her. But that was two days ago. Two long, confusing days she'd spent trying to evade the world at large.

What if they had damaged their friendship?

Arrggg. Everything was going down the shitter one flush at a…

"There you are." A dark shadow fell over Bailey, who was sitting Indian style on Cat's front porch. Covering her eyes, she looked up and let out a sigh of relief when she recognized Cat, peering at her with a frown. "I've been sitting in front of your apartment building for two freaking hours. Don't you know how to return phone calls?"

Bouncing up, Bailey stood with a smile. Cat seemed pissed but she was talking to her so that was something. "I'm here, aren't I?"

"Where were you two days ago?" Cat narrowed her eyes as she crossed her arms over her chest. "What the hell?"

Rolling her eyes, Bailey copied her stance. "Can we at least go into your house before we start the yelling? It's hot out here."

"Hmm…I should make you suffer." Pushing past her, Cat unlocked the door and gestured grandly for Bailey to enter. Once they were inside, Cat dropped her purse on the dark wooden floor and headed into the living room and straight to the bar.

Without saying a word, she made their usual drinks—vodka and tonic—while Bailey looked on. After handing Bailey her drink, they made their way over to the plush sofa and plopped onto it in unison as if it were an overstuffed beanbag. With legs tucked underneath them, they faced each other like gunfighters at the OK Corral, waiting for the other to make a move.

Neither one spoke for a moment. Both waiting for the other to talk first, and just as in high school, they both managed to start at the same time.

"Why are you avoiding me?"

"Sorry I've been avoiding you." The second the words left her mouth, Bailey burst into laughter. The amusing aspect of it all must not have been lost on Cat because she too started to laugh.

The sound of Cat's laughter was like a downy comforter to her. It filled Bailey with a sense of security and warmed her from the outside in. Everything was going to be okay. Nothing had changed.

"You first," Cat ordered, once she was able to get her laughter under control.

"That's fair." After taking a deep drink from her glass, Bailey began again. "I'm sorry I've been avoiding you, I was a bit freaked out by what happened."

"So in true Bailey fashion, you ran first and thought second."

Bailey ruefully smiled. "You know me so well. I'm sorry."

"Not good enough. You're not the only who was a bit shocked by the evening's entertainment."

The fact she wasn't the only person weirded out never crossed her mind, but of course she wasn't going to admit it. "With the things you write, I thought you might be a bit more adventurous than I first believed."

"Shut up."

"Come on, you guys started it."

"You didn't have to join in."

Not join in? It would have been easier to pluck her eyes out. "If I recall correctly, you were the one begging me to hurry up and do it so you wouldn't get another spanking."

Cat's mouth dropped open like a dead weight. "I cannot believe you said that."

"And I can't believe you let your husband spank you," Bailey added teasingly.

"I can't believe you liked it."

"No I didn't." Bailey fired back with a huge grin.

"Liar."

"Cyber slut."

"Lawyer fucker." The words were hardly audible over their infectious laughter. Tears of amusement streamed down Bailey's face as she fought to get herself under control. Lawyer fucker. Now she'd heard everything.

With a wheezed cough, Cat inquired, "So how was he anyway?"

"Un-fucking-believable. My orgasms had orgasms."

"That good?"

"Oh yeah." Bailey could hardly believe it herself. Who would ever have thought Sebastian could throw down like that? "We are so going to hell."

"As long as we get a single room with two couches, I think we'll all be okay with it."

They immediately broke out into laughter again and it seemed to go on forever. Just when Bailey thought she'd gotten herself under control, she'd look over at Cat and start again. They were so loud they missed the sound of the door opening and footsteps heading their way.

"Well…it looks as if we missed something." Mason's voice sobered the girls quickly.

Jumping from off the couch, they faced him and Sebastian like disobedient children. Bailey could feel the tip of her ears burning with embarrassment. From the knowing look in Sebastian's eyes, they'd been there for a while.

Didn't it fucking figure?

Her face glowed with embarrassment, making her more attractive than ever. They'd been talking about the voyeuristic night at the club. Sebastian might not have heard all of the conversation but he could tell by the looks on their faces the minute Mason and he walked into the room what the topic had been.

It was almost comical the way they acted. It was as if they'd been caught with their hands in the cookie jar. Sebastian watched Mason circle Catarena. Her stance never changed and for once Sebastian wondered exactly how far they carried the Dom/sub part of their relationship.

He made his way to where Bailey stood. She too was intently watching the other couple. Sebastian was sure she saw them in a whole new light now. He didn't think she'd ever really grasped the concept of what type of relationship Catarena and Mason participated in until the other night at The Boulevard.

"So, are you finished trying to avoid me?"

Bailey narrowed her eyes at him, a frown wrinkling her brow. "I was avoiding you. Three days' worth."

She was such a brat, always wanting to have the last word. Sebastian stepped forward, forcing Bailey to either back up or be run over. He kept at the slow but steady pace until they crossed the room and her back was pressed to the wall before leaning in to nip the side of her neck. "Only because I allowed it, Bay."

His words were arrogant and spoken only because he knew it would get a rise out of her. Any emotion, even anger, was better than nothing. Sebastian knew she was struggling through the intensity of what had taken place at the club. She was, more than likely, trying to deal with knowing her best friend was a freak, just as much as she was trying to understand how she could have so thoroughly enjoyed all that had happened.

She braced her hands against his chest. When she looked into his eyes, Sebastian felt heat wash down his spine to the base of his cock, lifting it until it throbbed. Being close to her by itself was enough to set him off but being close while dominating the situation nearly had him creaming his pants. What was it about bending Bailey to his will that kept Sebastian painfully hard?

"Don't be such an ass, Sebastian."

"How does telling the truth make me an ass?"

When Bailey pushed, Sebastian didn't back up. Instead, he leaned into her body, trapping her hands between them. "How, Bay? Tell me."

He couldn't keep his hands to himself. With her pressed between him and the wall, Sebastian wedged a knee between her thighs. Bailey gasped when he brushed against her sex for the first time. She whimpered with arousal when he angled his hips, adding pressure right where she needed it.

With her lower body pinned to the wall, he was free to use his hands however he desired. First he traced her face with his fingers, a hand at each cheek before sliding into the silky hair at her temples.

The control he felt was so erotic. It was one of the many reasons he'd never be able to enjoy a straight vanilla relationship.

"Tell me." Sebastian whispered the words against her lips.

"You can't make me do things I don't want to do, dammit."

She was a fighter through and through. Didn't she see just how strong the connection, the attraction, between them was? How could she deny it?

Sebastian tilted her head, positioning it just the way he wanted. The way he needed her so he could taste every dark recess of her mouth. When he nibbled at her full lower lip, she tried to pull away. The sting of his teeth holding her lip in their grasp stopped her immediately. Sebastian laved the small hurt with his tongue while Bailey moaned and wiggled her hips to get closer.

"Don't you see, Bay? Don't you see? When we're like this together, I could coax you into doing just about anything."

She of course stiffened at his words but Sebastian didn't let her reaction deter him. "But I don't want it to be this way. I want to make you so hot you want the same things I do. Not because I made you but because you wanted to. I want you to writhe beneath my hand, or belt even, because the burn turns you on. I want to see you tied to my bed because you love the way it feels to let go."

Sebastian laid his forehead against Bailey's, his eyes closed, breathing deep. "I'll push you, sweetheart, but I'll never hurt or force you." He opened his eyes. Staring straight into hers, he pushed away from the wall, separating their bodies. "The ball is in your court now, Bay. What are you going to do?"

She took a deep, shuddering breath. Then, just when Sebastian thought he'd finally gotten her, made her understand she was much more than just a fuck buddy, she popped off. "I'm going to stop letting you fuck me with them in the room."

Mason and Catarena, who were now sitting on the couch, evidently enjoying the show, both snickered.

Sebastian forced a smile, trying not to act as irritated as he felt. For the first time in his adult life, he wasn't sure whether to push the issue or not. There was no way he could just be her fuck-on-the-side, but then again, the thought of not fucking Bailey at all didn't sit well either.

"Well, this has been fun but I've got to go."

After saying her goodbyes to Catarena and giving a toodeloo wave to Mason, Sebastian walked Bailey to her car. Parked right out front, it made for a short trip. Once there, Sebastian pulled Bailey into his arms and kissed her, deep and slow. They were both breathless when he finally pulled his lips from hers.

"I'll pick you up at six tomorrow night? You pick the spot."

Bailey was shaking her head before he even finished the sentence. "I can't tomorrow."

"Why not?" Sebastian did his best not to sound like a petulant child. Bailey seemed wound tight. Her eyes looked everywhere but directly at him, giving Sebastian a bad feeling.

"Because I have a date."

Her words hit him like a sucker punch to the solar plexus and she knew it. She didn't seem to have a problem in the least with keeping a wall between them. Well, two could play at her little game.

"Okay. Well, I'll give you a call later in the week then." He kissed her again, a hard kiss this time. One to remind her of what she'd never get from some pansy-assed, vanilla lover boy.

She seemed shocked by his attitude. For a minute, she just stood there, staring at him. Sebastian helped her along by opening the door for her. Once she was comfortably seated behind the wheel, he reached in to pull her seat belt around her and buckle it before shutting the door.

"Drive safe." It was a lame thing to say, but at the time, was all he could think of. If he didn't get her out of there fast, he was going to drag her off to his house, tie her to his bed and whip her ass raw for even thinking of going out with another man.

With long, ground-eating steps, he stalked back to the house. Catarena and Mason were snuggling on the couch in their own little world but Sebastian didn't care. Shoulders tense with anger, he plopped his ass on the coffee table right in front of them.

"Who is Bailey going out with tomorrow night and where are they going?"

Catarena seemed surprised by his outburst. She looked from him to Mason and back. "She didn't mention it to me."

Sebastian turned to Mason. If anyone could get the information out of Catarena, he was the one.

"Oh no, you don't!" Catarena jumped to her feet, her hands fisted on her hips. "You asked me and I said I didn't know. Don't you dare give him your big puppy-dog-eyed look and get me into trouble."

Mason laughed.

"Okay. I'm sorry." Sebastian got up from his perch on the coffee table to pace across the floor before an idea hit him. "Does she have a favorite place?"

Catarena bit her bottom lip. She still stood with her hands on her hips, only now she didn't appear quite so confident. "Umm."

"If you know, I think you should tell him." Mason's voice was low but the hand he rubbed over the curve of her ass brought his point home.

"Yeah, as if I have a choice," Catarena muttered. "There's a place over on Fifth and Delaware where she likes to go. Good food and drink and a small dance floor but I don't remember the name."

Sebastian figured she was lying, but he knew the place she was talking about so wouldn't call her on it. Besides, by the way she and Mason were looking at each other, they would be having loads of fun the minute he walked out the door anyway.

"Thanks." He kissed Catarena on the cheek.

"I've got you," he murmured, thinking of Bailey as he made his way to his car.

Chapter Four

ഇ

Despite the pleased smile Bailey wore like a cheap toupee, she was having a terrible time on her date. While Darrel Hinx seemed like the perfect catch in theory, in reality he was a complete bore and a bit of an ass. Though to be fair, anything would seem tame compared to her last date.

Not that she could truly call her outing at The Boulevard a date. To be considered a date, one would have to do more than fuck someone in a room full of friends. Although if she wanted, she could stretch the evening out and pretend as if it were drinks and a show. A show involving spanking and bondage.

At the time she had agreed to the date with Darrel, Sebastian and she were still friends only. She was never one to date multiple men at once, even now she felt a sense of guilt being out with him, but it seemed rude to cancel a date just a few days before it was to occur.

Bailey was definitely in no mood to be out on a date with another man. She had just been kissing Sebastian yesterday, four days before she'd been impaled on his shaft. Hell, her body still had the impression of his fingers imprinted in small bruises on her thighs.

What really bothered her though, was the casual way Sebastian had told her to have a good evening. He said it as easily as he'd pulled her into his arms and kissed her senseless. Talk about a walking, talking contradiction.

Stop it, she scowled at herself. This night wasn't about Sebastian. It was about getting past him and she was never going to do it if she kept thinking about him.

"I truly think the hybrid is the car of the future. The gas mileage…" Though she nodded her head at the proper juncture, try as she might, Bailey couldn't focus on what Darrel was saying. In her defense, he hadn't stopped talking since he'd picked her up this evening so all of his words were beginning to blend into a humongous cloud of blah.

Handsome in an old-school Billy Dee Williams way, Darrel oozed charm and sophistication. Normally that was a good thing, but tonight it was a bit sickening. He seemed almost too perfect. And perfect was not a good thing. Especially when in her mind he was competing against the spanking son of Satan.

"Bailey?" Her name being called drew Bailey's attention back to Darrel. From the expectant look on his face he was obviously waiting for something, but for the life of her she didn't know what.

"I'm sorry." Bailey leaned forward and brushed her hand softly against his, flashing him a dazzling smile that was meant to distract him from her very palpable blunder. "It's a little crowded in here tonight, I didn't quite hear you."

"Don't worry about it." If his gaze had rested anywhere other than the top of her breasts, Bailey would have felt half bad. "For such a small restaurant, this place is rather packed. You would think the service and the food would be better."

Darrel was losing points left and right. Carmine's was Bailey's favorite Italian restaurant. "I think the service and the food are great."

"No, great would be *Clos de la Violette* in Provence." Pausing for dramatic effect, he took a long, slow drink from his wineglass. "Have you ever been to France?"

"No, I haven't."

"It's a beautiful place, so filled with beauty and art it almost takes your breath away. I should take you."

The urge to roll her eyes was great. He wasn't even going to take her on a second date, let alone out of the country. It was all an act and Bailey was more than aware of it. "Actually, I'm more of an India kind of girl."

"You don't want to go there."

"I don't?" The urge was back. Nothing irritated Bailey more than someone telling her what she wanted to do. It was bad enough she let Sebastian do it, but at least with him…damn it, she was doing it again.

She wasn't supposed to be thinking about him. She was on a date. With…with…Good Lord, what was his name?

"No, it's a very poor country."

"But rich in culture."

"Hmm…if that's what you want to call it."

What a glib ass.

Suddenly Bailey was okay with not remembering his name. They wouldn't be going out again so there was no reason for her to remember it. Taking a deep breath, she grabbed her wineglass off the table. Much more of his company and she was going to drink herself in a stupor just to get away from him.

As what's-his-face began to ramble on again, Bailey let her gaze wander over his shoulder to the couple walking toward an empty table. The man's back was facing her but there was something very familiar about his confident stroll, which kept Bailey's attention long past the point of decency.

It wasn't until after the gentleman pulled back the lady's chair for her to sit that Bailey noticed the gold heirloom ring on the man's ring finger.

No. He. Didn't!

Bailey sat straight, totally in shock. What the hell was Sebastian doing here? Better question, who in the world was the blonde with him?

Sebastian didn't even like blondes, at least she didn't think he did. He'd never mentioned liking them, but then again, he never said he didn't. Not that her hair was naturally blonde anyway. Bailey could see her roots clear across the room.

Stinky, stank, fake blonde.

"And I told my accountant…"

Oh my God, would you shut up, Bailey screamed in her mind. As if she really cared he had an accountant. She had a regular tax person at H&R Block, but she didn't go around bragging about it.

What was she going to do, besides stab Sebastian in the heart with his butter knife?

He had come here intentionally. Bailey was willing to bet anything on it. It was a low move, a vindictive, mean act. One he was going to regret for the rest of his very short, painful life.

As if sensing her stare, Sebastian looked up and right into her eyes. Bailey waited for him to acknowledge her with a nod, a wave or something, but he didn't. He just let his gaze wander over her and on to the next table, as if he didn't even know her.

Two could play his game.

Bailey turned her attention back to her date, convinced if she stared at him long enough she would remember his name. When he said something she assumed was supposed to be humorous by the way he chuckled, she laughed loudly and gaily, intent on showing Sebastian she could have a good time. Even though she wasn't.

Maybe she would take Darren…no Darrel, that was it, to The Boulevard. But just as quickly as the thought entered her head, Bailey vetoed it. She could barely remember his name, she definitely didn't want to see his freaky side.

Encouraged by her newfound interest him, Darrel leaned forward and brushed the back of his hand down the side of her cheek. "You have the prettiest smile."

And it was getting increasingly harder to aim it toward him. His touch left her cold. Only further driving home the point she shouldn't have been there. Worse yet, Sebastian either wasn't noticing or he didn't care.

"Thank you." Easing back in her chair, Bailey tried to subtly move away from his touch but keep her body turned in his direction so it appeared as if she was devoted to his attention.

"Are you ready to go?" Darrel asked, signaling to the waiter to come over.

"More than ready." Ready to get out of the restaurant, ready to get rid of Darrel, ready for this entire horrible night to end.

From the corner of her eyes, she saw Sebastian rise from his chair. For a split second Bailey thought he was going to come to her table to put an end to the silly, silent pissing contest they were having but he didn't. Instead, he walked down the aisle and to the back of the restaurant where the restrooms were located.

How could he go to the restroom at a time like this? Pushing back her chair, Bailey was halfway out of her seat when Darrel sharply called her name.

"Where are you going?"

Good Lord, was he still there?

"I have to visit the powder room before we leave. Excuse me for a moment, please." *While I murder my not-a-boyfriend,* she added silently to herself.

Lying Bailey over his lap and blistering her ass with the flat of his hand was too gentle a punishment in Sebastian's opinion. Witnessing her antics, the way she was hanging all over her date, made him livid.

The fact he'd asked Trista out and was forced to listen to her irritating, mindless giggles all night was Bailey's fault. It boggled Sebastian's mind just thinking about how many times he'd taken the other woman out, playing the scenes or just to have a trophy on his arm, and never once realized what a ditz she was.

Damn Bailey anyway for opening his eyes to all the dead-end dates he'd managed to muddle his way through over the years. And now, now he'd finally realized just what it was his life was missing, she had to go and play hard to get.

Didn't she understand how serious he was about a possible future between the two of them? Granted, he may not have been the first one to make a move, but now it was made and he sure the hell didn't intend to just pack up and walk away. Leaving Bailey, his woman, in the hands of some snotty-assed pretty boy just because she felt more comfortable with the type wasn't going to happen.

Sebastian stalked past a man leaving the now-deserted men's restroom. Once through the door, he went straight for the sink where he splashed cold water on his face.

"You'd better get your ass together before you go back out there and make a fool of yourself," Sebastian mumbled to his reflection in the mirror over the sink.

After drying his hands and face, he made his way to the urinal. He was just zipping the fly of his trousers when the door to the restroom opened. Since he was paying no attention to whomever it was walking through the door, Sebastian nearly jumped out of his skin when he turned around to see Bailey standing there.

"Bailey! What in the hell are you doing in here?" God she was a handful! Fighting the urge to just pull her into his arms, Sebastian made his way back to the sink where he proceeded to wash his hands while watching Bailey in the mirror. When finished, Sebastian stalked toward her until he was close enough to gently but firmly grasp her by the elbow.

He intended to escort her out of the men's room but she dug in and refused to budge. Other than bodily lifting her to accomplish the task, Sebastian was stuck. Bailey being Bailey, jerked her arm from his grasp. She took a step back, planted her fists on her hips and gave him a disgusted look.

"Damn, you guys are pigs." Her nose was wrinkled in a clearly "this place smells" way. She evidently realized she'd let her mind wander because her gaze snapped back to his, her frown once again in place.

"I can't believe you brought that blonde bimbo here and then…and then you have the nerve to ignore me. To act as if you haven't got a damned clue who I am. How rude! You didn't even say hi!"

She was breathless when she finally finished. Jealousy rang out clearly in her voice and her choice of words. Sebastian wanted to smile but he couldn't just yet. He had to play the part.

He closed in on her until they stood eye to eye. "You were the one who couldn't go out with me because you had a date. Remember?"

"Yeah," she interrupted him, "but I didn't say anything about you following me."

"Following you?" Sebastian tried to act nonchalant.

She rolled her brown eyes at him. When she leaned closer, barely brushing her lips against his, Sebastian had to remind himself where they were. Her change of tactic threw him for a loop. First she was pissed and now she was kissing him. Sebastian wasn't sure he even understood women.

"You know you brought your date here because this is where I like to come. Were you jealous, 'Bastian? Did it bother you I might take Darrel home after dinner and have my wicked way with him?"

She was taunting him. Teasing with words that made him want to punch Darrel's face and paddle her ass after he tied her to his bed.

"No, Bay, I wasn't worried." He lied through his teeth.

Her lips grazed his again, their warmth beckoning. "And why's that?"

"Because I know after the other night you realized there is no way a missionary screw in the dark can get you off the way I did." Sebastian nipped at her mouth as a reminder of the way he enjoyed his women.

His words were crude yet true. Bailey's eyes widened as the truth hit her. She didn't seem too thrilled. "You wish," she sneered. As soon as the words left her mouth, she spun on her heel and disappeared through the door.

"No fucking way," Sebastian muttered as he followed Bailey.

She'd only made it as far as the door to the ladies' room when he caught up to her. "Two can play at this game, sweetheart."

Sebastian grasped the handle with one hand and used the other to pull Bailey into the ladies' room behind him. "I always wondered what these little sitting rooms were for," he said, looking around at the cushy chairs and long countertop complete with a lighted mirror behind it.

With deft fingers, he locked the door. Once accomplished, he pulled Bailey into his arms. He speared a hand through the thick locks of her hair and tilted her head to receive his kiss.

There was nothing romantic or gentle about the way he took charge. Sebastian kept up the dominating kiss until she melted against him. Her moan of frustration sang through his mind as he gentled the kiss and allowed his hands to wander the length of her curvy body.

His need to taste her, to feel the warmth of her pussy was nearly overwhelming. Jerking himself away from the haven of her body made his cock protest but Sebastian had a plan.

With a few simple twists and untucks, Sebastian had his tie off and the first button of his shirt undone.

"Wh-what are you doing?"

Sebastian smiled, a crooked, predatory smile Bailey must have recognized if her widening eyes and look of wariness were any indication.

"Put your hands behind your back, sweetheart."

"Huh?"

"Bondage is damn near as exciting as spanking, don't you think?" It was a rhetorical question, not one he actually expected an answer to. "Since spanking you here might cause a scene, I thought I'd tie you up and for your punishment eat your pretty pussy until you pass out."

She visibly stiffened at his choice of words. "Punishment! Punishment for what?"

She was so damned sexy she made his balls ache. Even when she was being a brat, she had him twisted around her pinky finger.

"Punishment for even thinking you might give to someone else what belongs only to me. Now put your hands behind your back before I change my mind and spank your luscious ass."

He was going to die. His cock was so hard, Sebastian was sure it was going to burst. Just the thought of tasting her made his mouth water. Admittedly, he was a bit surprised when she turned around and presented her back and both hands to him.

With a minimum of effort, he looped his tie around her wrists, binding them loosely together so she could easily get free if she so chose. There would be another time, a more private time, to take the bondage side of their relationship to a whole new level.

Once she was facing him again, Sebastian grasped a hold of the spaghetti straps holding the chocolate brown confection of her dress up and pulled them down her arms until her pert, unfettered breasts sprang free.

"Beautiful. Now, let's see the best part." Sebastian lifted Bailey in his arms, loving the way her body, her bare breasts, felt against his cloth-covered chest. She was warm and so soft he could barely breathe.

He carried her to the long counter then sat her on its smooth surface. "Lift up," he ordered. When she did so, he lifted the hem of her dress until it was settled in a puddle at her hips. With a hand on each knee, Sebastian parted her legs. As sexy as her black thong panties were, they had to go. They hugged her silky dark skin so erotically Sebastian was almost sorry she'd have to lose them.

"Lift up again, sweetheart, let's get rid of these."

Bailey's eyes were closed, her lips slightly parted. She looked like a fallen angel. Sebastian removed his glasses then knelt between her splayed thighs. "So pretty," he whispered against her heated core as he pulled her panties free of her legs.

One swipe of his tongue and Sebastian was lost. Lost in her taste, in the way her body moved and the sexy sounds she made. But most of all, he was lost in her. Out of nowhere this woman had blindsided him and now, more than ever, he realized how much she meant to him. It was time to play hardball. Time to make her realize exactly what it was they could have together.

His thumb on her clit urged her on, pushed her closer to the precipice. "Oh 'Bastian."

"Mmmm," he hummed against her nether lips, sucking one into his mouth while playing with her clit. "What is it, sweetheart?"

"I need to come. I'll do anything, just please make me come."

Sebastian kept control of her body, holding her on edge by circling her clit. He stared into her face, searching her now opened eyes. "Get rid of your sorry excuse for a date and come home with me tonight, Bay."

She was shaking her head when Sebastian dove back in and sucked her clit just hard enough to make her buck against his mouth before pulling away. "O-okay. Whatever you want, just fuck me already. Make me come."

He was an asshole. A jerk of the worst kind and Bailey was surely going to let him know it, but what she wouldn't do is go back on a deal. It was one of her pet peeves. Sebastian knew it and used it as well as her sexuality against her. He should be shot. He felt guilty but not guilty enough to quit.

"My way. All night." Sebastian thrust two fingers deep into her quivering sheath then held still. With her hands tied behind her back, Bailey had no way to take what she needed.

"Bastard."

"I know, baby. Was that a yes?" He was going to hell. Shit, the Devil himself was probably taking notes.

"Yessss," she hissed between her teeth as Sebastian moved his fingers and worked her clit, sending her over the edge.

Sebastian was the Anti-Christ and she was a first-class harlot. Together the two of them were going to burst hell wide open. Bailey had done some lowdown things in her life but this probably took the cake.

She was working on feeling bad about it. Any second now she was going to give a damn. Yep, any second now.

With a smile she couldn't suppress, Bailey opened her eyes lazily and peered around the room. Life was good. She was floating in an abyss of bliss, quite content to sit bare-assed on the counter with Sebastian kneeling between her legs. He looked good there. In fact, it seemed rather fitting. Him before her, committed to pleasing her for all eternity. The imagery was something she could definitely get used to.

The jingling of the door handle abruptly pulled her from her euphoric high. "Hello. Is anyone in there?"

"One second please." Struggling to sit, Bailey wrestled with her silk constraint, desperately trying to free her hands. The homemade binding fell away quickly, a lot quicker than Sebastian, who was slowly getting to his feet. "Move!"

Jumping off the counter, Bailey struggled with her dress, pulling it back in place and slipping it down her flushed body.

What had she been thinking?

This was so embarrassing. Another prideful encounter for The Book of Bailey.

"Is there just one restroom?" The curious voiced called through the door.

"No…" Bailey threw her hands up in despair, desperately trying to think of something to say.

Unfortunately for her, Sebastian didn't seem to be at such a loss. "We were using the table. We'll be out in a minute, lady."

"Oh my!"

"Sebastian!" Plopping her hand over her mouth, Bailey turned back toward the door, afraid her outburst was going to bring the cops running. She was never going to be able to come to the restaurant again. It was a real pity. They had killer angel hair pasta.

"What?" The humor in his voice was unmistakable as he slid his glasses back into place. Then again, he was fully dressed and not damp between his thighs.

"What do you mean 'what'?" she whispered furiously. Shaking her head in frustration, Bailey turned back toward the counter so she could fix her disheveled appearance. Leave it to a man to be so blasé about everything. "Never mind. I'll give you a call later on tonight."

"I don't think so."

His comment brought Bailey up short. That wasn't exactly what she'd been expecting him to say. "Excuse me."

Sebastian faced her with a frown. All traces of humor had vanished from his face. "You have five minutes."

"To do what?"

"To go out there and get rid of him."

Startled, Bailey starred at him in shock. "How am I supposed to do that?"

"Blow him off, Bailey, you're good at it."

Bailey's face filled with heat. "Fuck you."

"Don't worry. You will." Bending over, he picked up her discarded panties and tucked them in his trouser pocket. "If he doesn't leave in five minutes, I'm coming over there and sending him on his way."

Bailey snorted. "You and what army?"

"I don't need an army, Bay." Sebastian took out her recently pocketed panties and dangled them in front of her. "I've got these. And if you don't have your pretty ass in front of the restaurant waiting for me, I'm going to stop by your table and drop them in his lap."

"You wouldn't," she gasped, grasping at her underwear in a futile attempt to take back the upper hand.

Sebastian snatched them out of her reach with a wicked grin. "Watch me."

"Bastard." Bailey bit back the words as Sebastian unlocked the door and opened it to the stunned woman still waiting outside.

The woman quickly looked between the two of them before muttering under her breath and dashing into one of the stalls. Sebastian grinned unabashed as he headed out the door, shoving her thongs into his back pocket as the door swung shut behind him.

"Fuck!" Bailey bellowed, mad she'd let things go so far. Sebastian was a dead man. A walking, talking dead man, and it was going to be a pleasure to put him out of her misery.

With the thought of his mangled corpse in mind, Bailey disappeared into a free stall and cleaned up the evidence of their little tryst. Ever mindful of the time, she quickly washed her hands before dashing out of the restroom, wanting to reach Darrel before Sebastian got to him.

To her ever-loving relief, the table Sebastian had been sitting at was empty. All traces of him and his date were gone. Too bad she couldn't say the same for her own table.

Darrel was still sitting by the table but he wasn't there alone. Somewhere between the argument and the oral sex he had picked up a little admirer in the form of their waitress, who was laughing gaily at something he had said.

Bailey was sure it was a fake laugh. Darrel hadn't said anything interesting or amusing all night. As far as she was concerned though, it wasn't a big deal. The waitress could have him for all she cared. More power to them.

The waitress spotted her before her date did and quickly made her leave. By the time Bailey was back at the table, Darrel had already stood, fake smile in place. "Are you okay? You were gone for an awfully long time."

"Actually I'm not," Bailey lied without batting a lash. "I was feeling a little ill," *from being caught with another man in the restroom*, "I think I'm going to just head home."

Frowning, Darrel nodded in understanding. "I told you the food wasn't great."

"It's not the food."

"Let me take you home."

Before she could reply, Bailey spotted Sebastian in the entryway of the dining room. Acting quickly, she grabbed Darrel's arm and spun him around until his back was toward Sebastian. "NO!" She practically bellowed. "I called a cab and they should be here by now."

"A cab? I really don't mind."

"I know, but it's okay." This was much easier when he was being an ass. Now she felt bad.

"Are you sure?" As he asked, the waitress strolled by again and his eyes followed her as she walked past them.

The guilt was gone.

"No, I'm sure. Thanks for an…" Bailey paused, searching for the right word. "Evening out. It was real."

"We should do it again."

He still wasn't looking at her, which made what she said next all the more easier. "No, we really shouldn't."

As he turned startled eyes back to her, Bailey picked up her purse and walked around him.

As she passed by Sebastian, he muttered, "It's about time."

Rolling her eyes, Bailey continued out the door and into the cool night air, only stopping when she reached his car. "Where's your date?" she asked as he leaned forward to open the door for her.

"You're my date."

Bailey sat in the passenger seat and waited until he walked around and got into the car before she spoke again. "We're two really fucked-up individuals. You know that, right?"

"That's why we're perfect for each other," Sebastian teased as he smiled.

Unable to help herself, Bailey started to laugh.

For a minute, Sebastian wondered why Bailey couldn't be as easily dealt with as Trista. Of course, the woman was only there because she knew she'd get a good meal and had high hopes of being ravished in bed afterward. The minute he'd picked her up, Sebastian regretted the decision.

Everything had turned out perfectly fine though. Not prone to clinging, Trista had merely stomped her foot in outrage and hailed a cab when he'd broken the news to her he wouldn't be taking her home. Now that she was gone, he could get back to what was really important.

Sebastian considered himself very fortunate Bailey hadn't told him off and bailed. He was a jerk of the worst kind for stealing her panties, even if they were drenched because of him.

Of course being the lawyer he was, Sebastian made his life out of winning arguments. He could be a self-righteous jerk above and beyond most, but if it got him what he wanted, then so be it. And right now he wanted Bailey. He wanted her in a way he'd never wanted another woman. She was truly bewitching him.

Sebastian waited before starting the car. The sound of Bailey's laughter was husky. The way she looked at him only made the ache in his groin worse. If he didn't do something to regain complete control of the situation, he was going to lose it. As far as he was concerned, there was nothing worse than a callous man who got his rocks off leaving the woman behind.

No, Sebastian wouldn't allow such a thing to happen. In the ladies' room, he'd had Bailey so hot and wet, she'd have agreed to anything, and her agreement to all of the wickedly kinky sex acts he could come up with was exactly what Sebastian wanted.

Because the Devil only knew, he had a hellaciously long list of things he wanted to do to her. With her. For her. There were more than likely sexual barriers stacked a mile high around Bailey. Sebastian planned to annihilate every damned one of them before they were through.

"'Bastian?" Bailey's voice pulled his mind from its one-way trip to the gutter. "Wasn't there someplace you wanted to take me or were we just going to sit here with you staring out the windshield, strangling the steering wheel all night?"

She was teasing him. Damned if it didn't feel good. Sebastian chuckled. "Oh yeah, baby. There is someplace I want to take you. But first..." he let his voice trail off as he leaned closer, inhaling her womanly scent.

Reaching across Bailey's lap, Sebastian reached for the hem of her dress. With both hands on her knees, he slowly inched it up until her legs were bare from mid thigh down.

"Mmm, much better."

Her cheeks were flushed. Her pupils dilated. She was obviously aroused, just the way Sebastian wanted her. He wanted Bailey to think of nothing but how badly she needed to come. He wanted her so primed and ready when he finally took her, she would beg for the slight stinging pain the flat of his hand would bring.

Sebastian started the car with the twist of his wrist. With one hand on the steering wheel and the other on Bailey's knee, he pulled away from the curb. "Open your thighs for me, sweetheart. I want to smell the sweet scent of your sex all the way home."

Her hands came forward, as if to cover herself from his gaze.

"Uh-uh," Sebastian tsked. "Now put your hands under you, sit on them if necessary, but don't cover yourself from me, Bay. Ever."

Hesitantly, she did as he asked. Sebastian tilted the rearview mirror so he could see her reaction. When the pink tip of her tongue peeked out to moisten her lower lip, he tightened his grip on her knee before repositioning the mirror so he could clearly see her lap.

"Pervert." There was a hint of humor in the single breathy word.

"You have no idea, Bay. None whatsoever."

"I think I'm starting to figure it out."

Sebastian's gaze jerked to hers. He wasn't sure what it was he heard in her voice, but he would find out. Knowing what she was thinking, what feelings were coursing through her body, was extremely important.

"So you are. And now that you have it figured out, is there anything you want to talk about? Any questions you want to ask?"

She shook her head before answering. "I'm just along for the ride, and from the looks of it, it's gonna be a helluva good one."

He couldn't help but smile. Just about the time he was sure she would insist he take her home, Bailey surprised him. It immediately made him wonder just how far he could push. Would she allow him to do more than loop his tie around her wrists?

Sebastian longed to bind her good and proper, to set her on a straight-back chair and work magic with his ropes. The contrast of her dark skin and the white of his favorite set of bondage ropes would be more erotic than anything he'd ever had the pleasure of seeing.

Would knowing she would be at his complete mercy set her off? It would be amazing to see just how little it would take to get her to climax. A good spanking, a good bit of bondage and the touch of only a feather perhaps? Or would she need more? Sebastian was ready to find out exactly what it would take. He'd test her limits and find all the secret little places that set her off.

"You're doing it again," she said, nodding to where his white-knuckled hands grasped the steering wheel. "How many times have you had to have it replaced?"

Sebastian arched a brow when Bailey giggled. Breathing a sigh of relief to finally have made it to his place without losing his mind or killing them both, Sebastian stopped the car and threw it into park.

He turned to Bailey. "Not my fault, sweetheart. It seems you are a distraction of the worst kind and I think I'll have to punish you."

She sputtered but couldn't seem to get a word out. It was shocking actually. Sebastian couldn't remember ever seeing Bailey speechless. "Don't worry, baby, it'll be part of the helluva good ride you were talking about."

He winked then climbed from the car. It took only a couple of seconds to walk around and help Bailey from the passenger seat. There was no way he could wait to kiss her.

His front door might only be a few yards away, but he had to taste her now.

"You make me crazy, sweetheart." It was a confession, one up until now Sebastian had never made to a woman before.

"Just being close to you makes me hard. Your scent, the way you scrunch your nose when you're thinking, it all makes me crazy to have you." He whispered the words against her lips, trying with all his might to keep the kiss slow and sensual when what he really wanted to do was devour her.

When she sucked his tongue into her mouth, Sebastian's cock throbbed in need of relief. Even as their tongues mingled and their lips pressed ardently against each other, his mind wandered to another time, another type of kiss.

Remembering the feel of her lips wrapped tightly around his cock sent fingers of fire licking up his spine. His damned cock was so hot. Hot, hard and thick. Sebastian was sure he would never make it into the condo before sinking every inch of his length deep within the vise-tight channel of her pussy.

With a shuddering sigh, he broke their kiss, pulling his mouth from hers. "We'd better go inside before I bend you over the hood of the car and fuck you until you can't walk straight."

"And that would be bad because?"

Sebastian smiled at Bailey. She had no idea just how close to the edge her sexy little spitfire self drove him. "Because if we got arrested, you'd never get tied to my bed and spanked the way you're creaming to."

With the flick of his wrist, Sebastian landed a playful swat on the full curve of Bailey's ass before he grasped her hand and led her to the door. It was going to be a window-steaming fuck-a-thon of a night if he had anything to say about it. And then, Bailey would give up all pretense of him being just a fuck buddy.

Chapter Five

ଛ

Butterflies were break dancing in Bailey's stomach as she walked through Sebastian's door. Despite her outer façade, she was a bundle of nervous energy ready to go off at any time.

The laughter, which had flowed easily between them in the car, seemed to be a thing of the past as they stood in his darkened condo. Every step took her farther into his living room, took her further away from her comfort zone. Everything had been great when they were just friends. But the more they got into the intimate side of their relationship, the more confused she became.

Never in her wildest dreams would Bailey have thought he would turn out to be such a complication. If they would have just had regular old, pump-twice-then-you- come sex, everything would have been fine. She would have gotten laid as she wanted and things could have continued on as they were.

Bailey should have known better. Things were never what they really seemed with Sebastian. Mr. Dependable was turning out to be this undercover, ass-whipping, panty-ripping addiction Bailey wasn't sure she wanted to be cured of. And that small piece of reality is what frightened her most of all.

With her back to him, Bailey faced the hallway, wondering if she should be bold and just walk into his bedroom. The words "my way, all night" reverberated in her mind like a broken record.

What exactly was his way and would it really take all night?

The sound of Sebastian's keys clinking in the glass bowl he kept near the front door broke the hypnotic gaze she'd developed staring into the hallway.

Clearing her throat, Bailey tried for flippant sass since her badass routine didn't seem to get her very far with Sebastian. "A real gentleman wouldn't hold a lady to a bargain made while she was under the influence of…well, you."

"On that note," his voice came closer as he stopped behind her, "a real gentleman wouldn't have gone down on you in a public restroom. I'm no gentleman and you're not getting out of this."

A smile flitted across her lips. Bailey moved to face him but was brought up short by his next words.

"Don't turn around," Sebastian ordered quietly. Gathering both wrists in his hand, he gripped her firmly and tugged her back against his hard body. "Tonight, we do things my way. The only words I want to hear from your pretty little mouth right now are 'yes' or 'no'."

Well damn. Bailey didn't think she'd ever get use to the Dr. Jekyll, Sexy Mr. Hyde side of Sebastian's personality. One second he was full of jokes, teasing her until she damn-near peed her pants laughing so hard and the next, he was giving her orders in the sexiest voice possible. The worst part was, she wasn't sure which side she liked best.

"Do you understand me, Bailey?"

"Yes." Bailey trembled at his words.

"This is the last opportunity I'll give you to back out. Once we move into the bedroom, all bets are off. I'll take you at my discretion. What I say will be law. Do I make myself clear?"

Was he kidding? Hell yeah, she understood. She understood and much to her surprise, she couldn't wait to obey. "Yes."

"Do you want to continue?"

If he really wanted to know, all he had to do was to slip his hand between her legs and feel the moisture gathering between her overheated thighs. "Yes."

"And I can fuck you any way...anywhere I choose?"

"Yes." This time it wasn't just her body trembling, her words came out a wavering mass of mush as well.

"Then come with me." Sebastian released his grasp on her wrists and instead took her hand into his. Without saying a word, he led her down the hall to his large master bedroom.

Bailey had been in his bedroom before but this was the first time she had been in there with the intention of anything carnal. Now, faced with the metallic headboard, which before had seemed a bit feminine to her, Bailey eyed the curved metal bars in a new light. Sebastian apparently hadn't been going for stylish—practicality evidently was his uppermost concern.

She moved forward to caress the footrest, a smaller mirror image of the headrest, but stopped when she spotted white binds laid out over his black Asian-printed quilt.

Ignoring his order to remain silent, Bailey sarcastically asked, "Should I assume these were for the dessert part of your date?"

Anger filled Bailey at the thought of Sebastian playing his bondage games with anyone other than her. Her anger was ridiculous but it was how she felt nevertheless. Bailey had never played or shared well with others and she was too old now to learn how.

Instead of the blast of anger she had hoped for, Sebastian remained cool, a bit too cool for her liking. With a tiny shake of his head, he walked toward her, stopping when they were mere inches apart. "Those were bought, ironed and laid out on the bed for you and you only."

"What if I hadn't come back here with you? Would you have let blondie take my place?"

"Does it matter?" Sebastian spoke softly as he slid the thin strap of her dress off her shoulder and down her arm. "We're just fuck buddies, right?"

With a gasp of surprise, Bailey reacted instinctively and brought her hand up to slap his face. As if he had been waiting for that exact reaction, Sebastian grabbed her hand in midair and spun her around. Trying to catch her balance, Bailey reached out blindly and grabbed hold of the bed, leaving her ass upturned in the air.

"Ah, ah, ah, brat." Sebastian growled as he pressed his erect cock against her from behind. "That's not the kind of hitting we do around here."

Bailey knew his intent before he acted on it. Before she could utter a word of protest, Sebastian stepped back from her, replacing his erection with a stinging blow from his hand.

"And I told you not to speak."

"Bastar—"

Smack! "You're not listening, brat. Yes or no only. Do you understand?"

Bailey refused to answer.

Smack! "I said, do you understand?"

"Yes." *Damn you*, she added silently in her head.

"Good." Sebastian ran his hands lovingly over her stinging flesh. His hands, warm and soft, continued with his earlier work, slipping up the slope of her back to her shoulders and then back down again, pulling the dress off her body as he went. His lips followed slowly down the trail of fire his hands started, kissing every inch of her newly bared flesh. Just when he reached her tender derriere, Sebastian pulled back. "Now climb on the bed like a good girl."

Doing as he asked, Bailey took her position in the center of the bed, lying back nude before his hungry gaze. Her ass might be tender but her pussy was wet. Talk about confusing. All this time when Sebastian had talked about spanking her, she'd thought, "hell no" but if those little swats were a testament of what his highhandedness could do to her body, then she was going to have to rethink her stance.

Bending forward, Sebastian picked up one of the restraints and ran it lightly over her sensitive breast. Bailey's nipple puckered under the attention and she clenched her legs together tighter to still the trembling running rampant through her thighs.

The corner of Sebastian's mouth crinkled at her body's involuntary reaction to him. "Do you trust me?"

"Sometimes," she answered honestly.

His brow rose high above the rim of his glasses. "Just sometimes?"

"Yes." She trusted him with her life, just not her heart. No one was deserving of that.

"Do you trust me to give you pleasure?"

"Yes."

"Give me your hand." Hesitantly Bailey placed her hand in his.

"The words 'no' and 'stop' can mean a world of difference in the heat of passion." Sebastian ran his thumb back and forth over the pulse of her wrist as he spoke. "So when you're bound for me, and trust me, you'll be bound for me often, I want you to use a different word. One if you utter, I'll know without a shadow of a doubt you want me to stop."

Wetting her parched lips, Bailey quivered before him. She wanted this. She wanted everything he had to offer. "What word?"

Sebastian raised her hand to his mouth and gently kissed her palm before bringing it over her head to the post of the headboard and securing it with the bind. "In honor of you, I want the word to be…buddy. As in fuck buddy. But since the word fuck sounds ever so sweet coming from your lips, we'll shorten it."

He studied her face, looking for any sign she might be uncomfortable with what was happening before reaching for her other hand. "And the other one?" When she lifted it to him, her fingers trembled slightly. Wasting no time, Sebastian secured her wrist to the opposite side of the headboard.

When she was bound to the headboard, her arms spread wide, Sebastian trailed a finger down her arm, over the protrusion of her collarbone and down her chest until his fingertip circled the peak of her bare breast.

Her skin was damp with perspiration, her tightened nipples gloriously dark in their aroused state. Taking his time was difficult when what he really wanted to do was sink the full length of his rigid erection between her tender glistening folds and pound her through the mattress.

With as much patience as possible, Sebastian circled her breasts with the same finger he'd used to explore her arm. She was warm and soft, just the way he liked his women.

And right now his woman was wriggling and moaning, trying to get his finger closer to where she wanted it. "Patience, Bay." He whispered the words a mere breath away from her ready and willing flesh.

Bailey opened her mouth to speak, to more than likely give some smart-ass retort, but stopped herself when he rolled her nipple between his fingers, adding just enough pressure to get her attention and hold it.

Her mouth snapped closed with an audible click. "I knew you'd be a quick study, sweetheart."

Sebastian lowered his head, taking her nipple into his mouth where he teased and tortured it with lips, teeth and tongue. He laved the area between her breasts, reveling in her taste and texture before settling over the turgid peak of her other breast.

"You're so beautiful, baby," Sebastian crooned, lifting his mouth from her now erect nipple. "And so responsive. I love the way your body responds to me."

Sebastian moved slowly up her body until they were face-to-face. He tangled his hands in the hair at her temples, holding her head still when she would have looked away, an embarrassed flush on her cheeks. "I'm going to play with you now, Bay. I'm going to taste every inch of your body and just when you think I'm done, I'm going to come so deep inside of you, you'll never forget how I feel. All of me."

Her eyes were wide and had gone from brown to deep amber. Sebastian covered her face with small, closed-mouth kisses before working his way down her neck where he suckled and licked the tender skin found there.

By the time he reached her navel, what seemed like an eternity later, his hands were also in the game. Sebastian changed the intensity of each kiss, each caress, keeping her a willing participant to her body's out-of-control responses.

What was once a gentle touch turned commanding just as his nibbling kiss became lustful and deep. "Nooo," Bailey cried out in protest when he pulled away. "Don't stop."

Her disregard for Sebastian's command to remain silent earned her a stinging swat to her outer thigh as a reminder of the rules.

"Mmmm," Bailey seemed to be enjoying their rough play. At least her hum of delight led him to believe so and since she hadn't actually spoken any words, he let it go.

Her body bucked beneath him, demanding release, urging him on when Sebastian was already too close to losing what was left of his control. His body was on fire, ready to explode. Seeing her naked and bound to his bed, the imprint of his hand on her flesh, was better than even the most erotic of dreams.

She was all he wanted and would ever need, if only she could see things the same way. Sebastian was determined to make a lasting impression, to take things just far enough so what had transpired between the two of them would haunt her nights and keep her wet and aching for him, for more.

A soft whimper of protest left her lips when Sebastian levered his body off hers and off the bed. "Watch me."

Spoken softly but still a command, he waited until he had Bailey's full attention before he began undressing. "Put your feet flat on the bed then relax. I want a clear view of what's mine while I'm undressing."

She hesitated for several seconds before moving her feet. Sebastian could clearly read the inner battle she fought in her eyes.

"You're beautiful, Bay. All of you. Now show me what I want to see or say your safe word."

Her eyes narrowed into dangerous slits at the no-nonsense tone of his voice. Sebastian pulled his leather belt from the loops of his trousers. "Unless you'd like a taste of what a real spanking is all about?"

Belt in hand, he took a step closer to the bed. As a man with a love for spanking, Sebastian had the kink down to an art. He'd spent years practicing with every implement available and making up a few as he went along. There was no way in the world he'd hurt her, but the thought of seeing well-placed stripes on her ass turned him on something fierce.

Evidently Bailey wasn't on the same wavelength. With her lips pressed together in a firm line, she relaxed her legs to the point her knees parted, leaving her sex gloriously open to Sebastian's heated gaze. The rapid rise and fall of her chest made her breasts quiver. The neatly trimmed triangle of hair covering her sex glistened with cream. Sebastian's mouth watered in anticipation.

With slow movements, he finished undressing. Even while taking his glasses off, he never once removed his gaze from her body. The folds of her pussy entranced him, beckoning him like a moth to flame. Sebastian had to taste her, to inhale her divine scent and feel her thick cream coating his fingers. It was no use. All pretense of being in control was heading straight out the window.

Sebastian made his way back onto the bed and without a word settled his shoulders between Bailey's thighs. With the first swipe of his tongue, her taste exploded in his mouth, overwhelming his senses. He was nearly out of his mind with need the first time she climaxed, the tight sheath of her cunt spasming around the fingers he had buried deep inside the warmth of her body.

More than anything, Sebastian wanted to feel himself enveloped inside her without the thin protective sheath of a condom. To feel the incredible heat of her body wrapped so tightly around him, flesh to flesh, would be like heaven and hell all rolled into one. It was something he'd probably never recover from and yet something he would never insist upon. A decision he couldn't make alone.

Using every ounce of willpower he had left in order not to throw himself on her and slam home, Sebastian retrieved one of the condoms he'd placed beneath the pillows and sheathed himself.

When he was finally settled between her thighs there was no going slow. All thoughts of gentleness and romance were gone. Every animal instinct lying deep within him had surfaced and was insisting he make Bailey his.

With a single thrust, Sebastian was buried balls-deep within the vise-like grip of her pussy. "Holy fuck!" She was tight and hot. He relaxed his arms, pressing her into the mattress as he came in for a kiss.

Sebastian felt the rapid beat of her heart against his chest. The sensation brought home the intensity of the moment. Deepening the kiss, he pulled back until just the head of his shaft remained inside the stretched opening of her pussy.

"Move with me, Bay. Tell me you want me." Sebastian broke the kiss to whisper the words against her temple. Placing his hands over hers, Sebastian entwined their fingers. He pumped his hips, thrusting and retreated at a slow pace, over and over again. The feel of Bailey's heels on his ass, urging him deeper, only added to the almost violent need coursing through his body. "Tell me."

When the tight sheath of her pussy pulsed around his cock, rippling with tiny pre-orgasmic spasms, Sebastian knew he wouldn't be able to hold back.

"Oh...damn! I want you, 'Bastian. I want you. God, I'm coming...oh!" Sebastian could feel the warmth of her tight sheath grabbing at his cock, trying to milk him of his essence.

"Damn, Bay, you feel so fucking good! Come with me, baby. Come for me." The last words were torn from Sebastian's throat as an orgasm ripped through his body, stealing his breath in the process.

Not usually one for cuddling and other post-orgasmic bliss, Sebastian found himself wanting nothing more than to do just that with Bailey. He wanted to hold her close, spooning her body with his until they drifted off to sleep.

Never before had he thought to awaken next to a woman and not mind the fact her mascara made her look like a raccoon or her breath was less than desirable. It was absolutely mystifying he wanted such things with Bailey.

The only problem was, Bailey was poker stiff beneath him and hadn't yet uttered so much as a word. After untying her, Sebastian moved off the bed to dispose of the soiled condom, only to find Bailey crawling from the bed, trailing the sheet behind her as he joined her on the bed once more.

"Where are you going?" Sebastian asked, climbing back into the bed. If Bailey thought she was going to tuck tail and run, she had another think coming.

Pasting a fake smile on her face, Bailey turned to face Sebastian. When she saw the way he was lying back on the bed, her stomach tightened with a need she thought long satisfied. With one leg stretched straight out and the other raised, Sebastian was the perfect picture of decadence. There was a lazy look in his eyes, which spoke of a satisfaction, which as silly as it sounded, made Bailey feel a bit proud.

He was just too much.

How she managed to stay out of his bed this long was a mystery even to her. Sure, he wasn't her normal pretty-boy type, but there was just something about him that made her catch her breath.

And the way he was stroking the white tie, the same tie he'd used only moments ago to bind her to his bed, wasn't helping matters in the least.

"To the shower, if that's okay." Arching a brow, she placed her hand on her hip, trying to get back into the sassy role she played so well. Her emotions were all out of whack, but it would do no good to let Sebastian in on her little secret. She had to be strong for her heart's sake. "Or do I have to ask permission?"

"No, you can shower. You just can't run."

Bailey rolled her eyes. "Run from what? We had a good time, now I'm going to clean up so I can go home."

"Home?" Sebastian sat up in the bed. All traces of relaxation were gone from his face.

Apparently, he had been expecting a different answer.

Oh joy. "Yes, you know, the place where I sleep."

"You can sleep here."

"No, I can't." Bailey said the words firmly, hoping he wouldn't push further, but she should have known better. Sebastian had never been one to let well enough alone.

"Why?"

Did he need only one reason?

With a mock growl, Bailey stormed over to the bed and hopped on it. Sebastian grabbed her in mid bounce, causing her to burst out laughing when he rolled over her, trapping her beneath his frame.

"Don't be so grumpy." Bailey brushed his hair from out of his eyes. The intimacy of the gesture and the way they looked at one another was a bit disconcerting. They had just made wild, crazy monkey love and yet one simple move was making her insides feel funny.

She stared in wonder into the deep green pools of his eyes. This was one of the first times she'd seen him up-close without his glasses on. It was almost like seeing him for the first time all over again. "I don't do sleepovers. Come on, 'Bastian, this is fun. Let's not ruin it by thinking it's more than it really is."

"And what is it, really?"

"Friends having fun."

Instead of the instant angry reply she'd been expecting, Sebastian merely nodded his head before dropping a kiss on her forehead. Bailey lay stunned on the bed when he released her without a word. It wasn't as if she wanted to argue about this again, she just didn't expect his quiet resolve.

Sebastian got off the bed and headed in the direction of his bathroom without saying a word.

"'Bastian," Bailey called out to him, their roles now completely reversed. "Where are you going?"

"To start you a shower, brat." Flicking on the light, he turned to her with a smile. "Why don't you relax while I get it going?"

Now it was her turn to frown. She wasn't relaxed at all. She was confused. Not as much by his casual attitude as much as she was by her irritation at his casual attitude. It took her a moment before it finally dawned on her what was so annoying about it. Sebastian was acting just as he had when she'd mentioned her date. Calm and completely at ease with everything she had to say. If tonight were anything to judge by, he wasn't to be trusted when he acted this way.

"Shower's on, doll." His words rang out from the bathroom.

"Doll," she echoed, frowning at his choice of words. Doll was a name reserved for Dolly Parton types, big boobs and platinum hair. She was a brat. His brat. And he damn well better not forget it.

Bailey dropped the sheet as she hopped from the bed, intent on giving Sebastian a piece of her mind, but was brought up short by the sight of Sebastian waiting in front of the haze-filled glass doors. The steam from the shower poured into the warm taupe room, surrounding Bailey in a heat-induced mist.

Sebastian's shower was larger than her entire bathroom, more than enough room for the two of them to bathe together. Although from the look in his eyes, bathing wasn't the only thing he had planned. Bailey's body reacted instantly to the desire and the promise of things to come pouring from his gaze.

Good Lord! How could she be getting aroused so soon? Her pussy still ached from their bout five minutes ago.

"Did you slip me an aphrodisiac when I wasn't looking?" Although her voice held a teasing tone within it, Bailey was partially serious. Never before had she reacted with such abandonment with anyone. The nonstop craving was going to drive her mad if she didn't get it under control and fast.

"Yes," he teased as he helped her into the shower. "I tongued it into your pussy at the restaurant."

"I believe it."

With a groin-tightening chuckle, Sebastian pulled her deep into the midst of his shower. "I think it's time for another dose, don't you?"

Sebastian closed the door behind her and stepped under the pouring water. He looked like a heathen water god—sexy, primitive and seductive. Needing to separate herself, if only in mere inches, Bailey stepped away from him until she was flush with the wall, needing something—anything—to keep her up straight.

When did he get so unbelievably sexy?

"Are you trying to kill me?" The cool tile against her back brought back a cold dose of reality, but it didn't last long. Bailey's nipples tightened as Sebastian lathered his hands with a bar of soap. "What are you doing, 'Bastian?"

"Making sure you go home as clean as possible." Sebastian placed the soap back in its dish and moved toward her with a seductive little smile. The second he touched her, Bailey knew she was in trouble.

His soapy hands slid along her body, lathering her with slippery fingers as he roamed her frame with ease. Every touch seemed innocent on the surface but the slow, sensual caresses inflamed her, drawing deep moans of approval and desire from her seemingly parched throat. Bailey had never been bathed so intimately and thoroughly in her entire life. She would have been a lot cleaner though, if it weren't for the juices flooding her pussy.

Once she was covered from shoulder to ankle in suds, Sebastian reached behind him and took the showerhead off the wall. He was as gentle as if washing a newborn baby, spritzing her entire body, rinsing her clean. His mouth soon followed the water trail. Sebastian kissed down her flat stomach, pausing to dip his tongue into her navel before settling between her thighs.

Gasping as he tongued her hot box, Bailey gripped her hands in his hair. "You have a pussy fetish?"

"No." Sebastian spread her lips apart, teasing her with a swipe of his tongue. "I have a Bailey fetish. But as tempting as this sweet pussy is, I'm not going to eat it."

"You're not?"

"No, this is about bathing, right?" Sebastian's words should have been a hint as to what he had planned next. Impatient for the feel of his tongue, Bailey leaned her head back against the tile wall and closed her eyes. But they soon popped open again at the first blast of water against her sex.

"What the...?" Her words were a garbled mess as Sebastian held firm the showerhead between her legs. The surging water pounded onto her clit, forceful and powerful. The constant pressure, both painful and pleasurable all at the same time, left her breathless and reaching out blindly for Sebastian.

But instead of coming to her as she wanted, Sebastian stayed on his knees in front of her, torturing her with the showerhead turned instant sex toy. Bailey had never satisfied herself this way before. The pulsating stream of water kept her on the edge of pleasure, moving too quickly to get her off, but keeping enough pressure on her she was constantly on the verge of orgasm.

"'Bastian." With a helpless sob, she responded to the pounding water, bracing her hands on his shoulders for support. The pleasure was almost too much but still he held steady. He kept the spout tilted, aiming the water directly at her erect button. Just when Bailey thought she would go mad from the lack of release, Sebastian moved the spot and replaced the water with his mouth, sucking her clit into his mouth, giving Bailey the extra pressure she so desired.

"'Bas...'Bas...'Bastian!" Her knees buckled as her orgasm ripped through her body.

Sebastian tortured her with his mouth a few seconds longer before dropping the spout and standing. He gently turned Bailey around until her breasts were pressed flush against the shower wall. Parting her thighs, Sebastian picked up one of her legs, and placed it on the ledge, brushing his cock against her tender lips. "You don't have to go just yet, do you?"

"No..." Bailey panted, pushing her ass toward him. She didn't want to go anywhere anytime soon. Not until she sated her hunger with him. "Not just yet."

"Good."

* * * * *

Sebastian checked his watch for what had to be the tenth time and each time he did, he received a scowl from the woman sitting across the desk from him. He was going to end up getting fired by one of his law firm's biggest clients if he couldn't gather his wits and stop thinking about Bailey.

Easier said than done, Sebastian decided two minutes and thirteen seconds later when he once again checked his watch.

He'd gone against every dominant bone in his body when he'd taken Bailey home the night before. She belonged with him, to him, and yet Sebastian hadn't been able to ignore the wide-eyed need in her eyes. Need for understanding and for space to think. It was the space part he was having a real hard time with.

Unwillingly he'd agreed, knowing if he pushed Bailey when it came to her feelings, it would only make matters a hundred times worse. She needed time and space but most of all, she needed to know he was willing to compromise.

It was the exact reason Sebastian hadn't called her the numerous times he'd picked up the phone. Instead, he'd made her promise to meet him for lunch. She was late.

"Are you paying attention to what I'm saying, young man?" At eighty-six, Mrs. Mabel Petersham was as sharp as a tack, a force to be reckoned with. She didn't take lightly to being ignored and was making her displeasure quite clear.

"Sorry, ma'am, I didn't quite catch the tail end of what you said." Or the beginning for that matter, but Sebastian wasn't on a professional suicide mission so he kept that bit of information to himself.

Mrs. Petersham sat across from him, her shocking white hair pulled back in a bun so tight it left her eyes slanted, unflatteringly showing the harsh angles of her face. Although she was an opinionated pain in Sebastian's ass, he had a soft spot for the old crone.

She'd been his very first client after passing the bar exam and had even followed him when he'd opened his own firm.

She was nosy and old-fashioned and somewhere along the line, had gotten the notion he needed a woman in his life and proceeded to lecture him about it every chance she got.

With as much nonchalance as possible, Sebastian once again peeked at his watch. The sound of Mrs. Petersham's cane thumping the floor at her feet caught his attention. He inwardly cringed when she opened her mouth for what was sure to be a lengthy lecture on his need for many fine sons when there was a knock at the door.

Sebastian released a huge sigh of relief and bid his savior, whoever he or she might be, to enter. The sight of Bailey's beautiful face as she peeked around the door brought a huge smile to his lips.

"Come on in, sweetheart." Sebastian rose from his seated position and moved toward her. Once close enough, he gathered her against him and proceeded to kiss her senseless.

It wasn't until Mrs. Petersham not so quietly cleared her voice that Sebastian remembered where he was. He was at work, a professional, and had a client in his office to boot.

"Damn." He thrust a hand through his hair as Bailey backed away from him.

"I...umm, can come back later." Bailey peeked over his shoulder and gave a little wave to Mrs. Petersham. "Just give me a call when you're done."

There was no way in hell Sebastian was going to let her go. As far as he was concerned, the visit with his client was over.

"No, but would you do a favor for me, Bay?"

Bailey took a couple of steps back before smoothing her skirt. "Sure." She kept her voice low.

"I've got some papers that need to go to Phil Marshall's office but my secretary is running an errand. Would you take them to him for me?" Sebastian leaned in close. Then lowering his voice, he added, "I'll get rid of Mrs. Petersham by the time you get back and then we'll go to lunch."

"Okay." Bailey reached up as if to touch him but stopped mid movement, choosing to fix his tie instead. Sebastian wondered if she realized how much more telling the little action was, even over a simple caress?

With Bailey headed for the door, Sebastian turned to once again address his client only to find her standing almost directly behind him and she actually had a smile on her weathered face.

"Now I see why you were so addlebrained today." She cackled, the sound grating on Sebastian's nerves. "She's a fine-looking woman and since you're not too shabby yourself, the two of you ought to make beautiful combo babies."

Sebastian, who had been heading for the door, stopped in his tracks. "Excuse me?" His voice was calm and decidedly cool, not at all friendly as usual. It was a tone that would have warned those who knew him well but Mrs. Petersham wasn't paying attention.

"My great-granddaddy had a baby with a colored woman. Of course, back in the day, it wasn't something you spoke of. I never met the woman who was his child but did see pictures of her. She was a beautiful mix of black and white. My mammie always said it wasn't polite to say so but I've always believed in speaking my mind."

If she had been a man and forty years younger, Sebastian would have laid her flat. He was so angry and offended, he couldn't quite think straight, which was the reason he said the first thing to came to mind.

"Speaking your mind doesn't give you leave to be disrespectful and downright rude. Our meeting is over, Mrs. Petersham, and until you can learn to leave your racist comments at home, I'd rather meet with another member of your family where your estate is concerned."

The old woman's smile slid from her pale face and for a moment Sebastian feared his harsh words might have been detrimental to her health. He was only glad Bailey hadn't been there to hear the ignorant woman's narrow-minded view.

The soft click of the door closing rang throughout the room like a gunshot. She had heard! Sebastian wanted to roar with anger, to curse and stomp at the unfairness of it all, but he wasn't a child.

Out of patience, Sebastian lowered his head and ran his hand across the back of his neck in an attempt to stop the threatening headache.

"Oh dear. I'm so sorry." Mrs. Petersham's voice wavered from behind him. "I can't seem to move with the times. I'm so sorry I offended. I'd like to say it comes from being raised by a racist bastard of a father but I'm old enough to know better. I want to apologize to your lady. It's the least I can do for not knowing when to keep my mouth closed."

Sebastian looked up in shock. It was the first time he'd heard Mrs. Petersham utter anything even remotely close to an apology. He gently took a hold of her elbow and escorted her to the door. "I'll make your apologies, Mrs. Petersham."

Mrs. Petersham made her way through the door at a snail's pace. "Yes, please do." She took a few more steps before turning back to him. "You are a good man, Mr. Emerzian. Because of folks like me, your time together will be even harder than normal but I don't see you as letting the little things get in the way. Nope," she shook her head. "You are not a quitter. Keep fighting and keep your girl on her toes. She looks to be a feisty one."

Sebastian closed the door behind the cackling old woman. He was still offended and still angry but not nearly as much as he'd been to start with. He moved back to his desk and for the umpteenth time checked his watch, wondering once again where the hell Bailey was.

Chapter Six

ഇ

Combo kids. Now Bailey had heard it all. Just thinking of the old woman's comment had Bailey shaking her head in a mixture of amusement and exasperation. As if there weren't a million different ways to describe mixed kids. Even if she didn't want to be PC, she could have come up with another phrase.

Yet, even though she was a bit taken back from the elderly lady's words, Bailey didn't have it in her to hold a grudge over something so silly. The woman was older than dirt. She probably thought it was a compliment of sorts.

Idiot.

Hearing the woman's uncouth description didn't surprise her as much as hearing Sebastian tear into the woman. He should have known better. He couldn't just go around biting off people's heads when they said something about their races. Stupidity was the way of the world and unfortunately Bailey had long ago given up on the world changing, not in her favor anyway.

It wasn't as if she was a pessimist or anything. In fact, she considered herself more of a realist and in reality, despite the propaganda Disney sprouted, it wasn't really a small world after all.

Bailey had never let anyone's opinion mar her own. She was a big girl. More than capable of forming her own beliefs and she didn't fault anyone for theirs, even when she didn't agree with them.

Anyway, she wasn't going to let anyone ruin her day. She hadn't gone to work today because it was a school day for her. The last day of school to be precise. Bailey was completely done with school. She had her degree and now she had her teaching certifications. Life was good and in a few months, she'd be able to quit her job with the smack-talking cow and go pursue her lifelong dream of teaching disabled kids.

Bailey strolled down the busy hallway with a song in her heart as she made her way to Sebastian's partner's office. Although she had been to Sebastian's office on many occasions, she had never had the pleasure of meeting Phil Marshall. Bailey had heard so much about the outspoken Texan she felt as if she already knew him.

If his secretary was there, she could just do a flyby. Hand the papers off to her, go rescue Sebastian...or the old woman, whichever one of them was in the most danger, and then 'Bastian and she could do lunch. Her treat.

Bailey looked around the empty outer office with a frown, now what was she supposed to do? The front desk was empty. Didn't it just freaking figure?

"Does anyone work here?" she grumbled as she walked past the empty desk. Tapping her fingers against the file, Bailey stood in frustration, debating on what to do. She could always just take the papers back to Sebastian and let his absentee secretary actually do her job and deal with it when she got back or she could leave them on the desk Phil's secretary was supposed to be occupying.

Eyeing the cluttered desk, Bailey quickly nixed the idea. Just her luck, they'd get lost and she'd be the one to blame.

"Fuck it." Just as she turned to leave the room, Bailey heard a deep chuckle from behind the closed office door bearing Phil's name in an elegant gold font.

Great, someone was in there. She could just hand them the papers and then bail. Pausing outside of the closed door, Bailey wondered what to do. She could hear a soft murmur from behind the door but she didn't just want to barge in. Then again, she didn't want to be here all day either.

Bailey knocked briskly on the door as she twisted the doorknob, pushing the door open. "Excuse me, Sebastian asked me...ummm..." The papers dropped to the floor as she brought her hand up to cover her mouth. There was someone in there all right. Her eyes widened as she got her first real glimpse of Phil.

What a glimpse it was. The tall, imposing man was standing near his desk in a very nice navy blue suit, or at least he was wearing the top half of the suit. His slacks were pooled around his feet and there was a woman kneeling in front of him.

Phil glanced toward the open door and cocked a brow as if to say, "Yes". Instead of pushing away from the woman who was working his cock like a pro, he entangled his large hand in her even larger bouffant blonde hair and pulled her down farther onto his penis.

His extremely freakishly large penis.

Bailey didn't mean to stare. Hell, she didn't even mean to still be in the room, but she was rooted to the spot at the sight of the largest cock she had ever seen. It was huge. How the hell was the woman even able to get her mouth around...

Phil's deep chuckle brought her gaze from his length to his grinning face. "Unless you're planning on joining in, lil darlin', I'd suggest you close the door."

"Oh my God. Sorry." Bailey turned her back to him, her face inflamed with embarrassment. She lowered her eyes to the floor where they rested on the papers fanned out over the taupe carpet. She was so not picking them up, but she was here for a reason. "Sebastian wanted me to drop those papers off."

"Well, tell him I'm much obliged. Now if you don't mind..." His voice trailed off as a loud slurping noise penetrated the air.

"OhmyGod. OhmyGod." Bailey's words ran together as she slammed the door behind her, leaning against it for a second until a husky moan had her catapulting across the room and down the hall. Of all the different ways she expected to meet Phil, barging in on him while some big-haired blonde went down on him wasn't on the list.

Bailey giggled all the way back to Sebastian's office. If she were his secretary, Bailey hoped the woman was getting paid time and a half for her dictation. She knew the image of the office rendezvous would be permanently etched in her brain.

How was she ever going to be able to look him the face? Oh hell, who was she kidding? She was never going to be able to look higher than his crotch again.

Murphy's Law ensured Sebastian's secretary Raya Cook was back at her desk by the time Bailey made it to his office. The pretty brunette smiled at Bailey as she entered.

"Mr. Emerzian said for you to go straight into his office as soon as you came back."

"Thanks." Bailey was still all smiles as she walked into Sebastian's office but she was the only one. Sebastian was wearing the fiercest scowl she'd ever seen. "Who peed in your Cheerios?"

"Are you kidding me?" Sebastian moved past her and slammed the door shut, quickly ruining Bailey's good mood.

"Look if this is about Phil, it was an accident."

"Phil, what are you talking about?"

"Nothing. What are you talking about?" Bailey redirected the question, in hopes Sebastian wouldn't ask for details. Knowing Sebastian as she did, this was probably something he wouldn't be too thrilled about. It was for the best if she kept the little episode to herself.

"Fucking old bat. I can't believe she had—"

"Whoa…" Bailey held up her hand, effectively cutting Sebastian off mid sentence. "What ol' bat?"

"Bailey." The way he dragged out her name meant only one thing. He was irritated, but for once Bailey had no clue why.

"What?" She raised her hands in confusion. "Did I miss something or what?"

"I know you overheard what she said, you don't have to pretend."

"Pretend…who's pretend…ohh." Is that what had him all in a tizzy? "That old lady's comment? Please, you can't still be upset about what she said."

Sebastian's narrowed gazed answered her question. "'Bastian, you're going to have to let stuff go, especially when it involves your clients."

"Former client."

"I don't think so." He was so fierce. How cute. "Look, if we're going to be friends…"

"Friends?" Sebastian crossed his arms over his chest and raised a brow sardonically.

Bailey rolled her eyes. She was not getting into this today. "Okay, special friends. You're going to have to get used to the looks and the comments. To tell you the truth, I thought the combo thing was kind of funny."

"It wasn't funny."

"It was, because she wasn't trying to be rude. Somewhere in her old decrepit brain she probably thought she was giving us a compliment. It's not as if we have to worry about kids or anything, but if combo is the worse thing interracial kids get called, consider it a blessing. As long as she didn't drop the N bomb, I'm cool. I mean, come on, it's probably not even the worst thing I've heard all day."

His scowl depended. "I'm not feeling better, Bay."

"Well, you should." Bailey appreciated he was upset for her but it wasn't necessary, racism was a part of her life and as long as he was in it, he'd was going to have to get used to it.

"You can't dismiss every client or fight every battle. You're just going to have to get used to it."

* * * * *

Sebastian stared at Bailey from across the table. They were seated in a cozy little alcove at a local diner waiting for their lunch to be served. The atmosphere was nice, his company was gorgeous and yet he couldn't seem to get a hold of his temper.

It was completely mind-boggling to Sebastian how Bailey could be so cool and seem so unaffected by what she'd heard.

"Stupid people aren't going anywhere, 'Bastian, so you might as well get over it. Ignore it. I do." Bailey's eyes shone with a wicked gleam and she laughed. "For the most part."

"I don't see how you can be so damned calm." He was frustrated and offended and so very sorry he'd managed to get Bailey into the situation to begin with. It was a good thing Mrs. Petersham was old and female. If not, Sebastian would have rearranged her face without second thought. He fisted his hands on the table, unable to keep his frustration from showing.

"If I became irate every time some ignorant yahoo spouted off, I'd never be anything but mad. A huge waste of time if you ask me."

Bailey had a very valid point. Sebastian unclenched his fists and inhaled deeply, pulling in her scent, her closeness. When he felt back in control, he placed his hand over hers and squeezed. "You're a better person than I am, sweetheart."

"Nope, I've just had more practice." There was no bitterness to her words and her smile let him know she really was okay with the whole thing.

Sebastian released her hand. Sitting back in his seat, he asked, "Well, now you've straightened me out on everything, what did Phil have to say when you dropped off the file?"

Bailey choked on the drink she'd just taken a sip of. Her eyes were wide and seemed to be settled somewhere around the area of his chest. Sebastian, who knew Phil well, let his mind jump to conclusions as to what could possibly have happened.

"Look at me, Bay." His voice was low, commanding. Bailey's gaze snapped to his. "Did Phil do something to make you uncomfortable? If he did, you'll tell me now."

Her eyes narrowed and she frowned. "I really hate it when you talk to me like that." She was obviously irritated and when Bailey was irritated, she wasn't likely to give him the information he wanted.

"It was an easy question, Bailey. Did Phil do or say something to you when you delivered the file for me?" This time Sebastian did his best not to push too hard. He tried with all his might to remain in control and nonconfrontational.

Bailey was shaking her head before he even finished the sentence. The tip of her tongue peeked out to wet her lips, a nervous gesture Sebastian was growing to love. He wanted to pull her into his arms and kiss her, to nip her full lower lip before sucking it into his mouth, but he wanted a damned answer even more.

"Sweetheart?" Alone it was an innocent word, but combined with the no-nonsense tone of his voice, it was a warning not many would ignore.

"He...uh. He wasn't alone."

Sebastian already felt better. If he knew his partner at all, there was more than likely a woman involved.

"Let me guess, you caught him chasing his secretary around his desk?"

Bailey did that little thing with her nose. The one where she scrunched it in concentration and damned if the little nuance of hers didn't have him rock-hard and aching.

"I'm assuming you have some type of professional dress code your employees are supposed to follow?"

Sebastian played along. Knowing Phil, this story was bound to be good. "Nothing specific, just your normal office protocol. Nothing too revealing, no jeans, you know the type of thing."

"Then she wasn't his secretary."

Sebastian couldn't help himself. There was just something about the way Bailey told a story that made him ask. "How can you be sure?"

Bailey gave an unladylike snort. Then in a conspiratorial way, she leaned forward. "I think it was the sequined dress and bouffant hair. I mean, I didn't get a look at the front of her though. Her dress could have very well been within your employee dress code but the way she was on her knees with her face buried in Phil's crotch made it hard to tell."

It was Sebastian's turn to choke. His drink nearly exited through his nose before he managed to swallow it. Grabbing a napkin off the table, he swiped at his mouth. "Damn, Bay, you've got to warn a guy."

"That ain't nothing. I'm sure I looked worse when I walked into the room. It took me a second to realize what was happening. Afterward, I was just mesmerized. It really was embarrassing though." Bailey took a sip of her drink. She waved her hand in the air as if to make her point. "Phil didn't even try to cover up. He told me to close the door. Here he was with a woman kneeling in front of him, blowing him, and he tells me to close the door."

She seemed to be gaining steam. Her movements were becoming more animated and her facial expressions were downright hilarious.

"And there I was with my jaw on the floor. Not because of what they were doing…" Catching sight of the waiter coming toward them, tray in hand, Sebastian missed a few words of Bailey's story. "…huge! I mean, I didn't know there were actually dicks as big as his out there."

The rattle of dishes announced the arrival of their waiter. His freckled face was red clear to his hairline. Bailey looked at the young man, a hand covering her mouth before turning back to Sebastian.

Her eyes were nearly bulging out of her head and from the way her shoulders shook, Sebastian would bet she was having a really hard time holding back a fit of giggles unlike any other.

"Will that be all?" From the look on the waiter's face, he was silently praying their answer was yes. Sebastian nodded to let the poor guy know they didn't need anything else.

"Damn, sweetheart, I believe you outdid yourself this time."

"Oh hell!" She was still laughing, and from the looks of it, she wouldn't be stopping any time soon. Bailey kicked his shin beneath the table, causing Sebastian to jump.

"Ouch. What did I do?" He kept an innocent look plastered across his face. It was times like these, silly conversations and laughter, that made Sebastian realize he could very well spend the rest of his life with the woman seated across from him.

"For not warning me. We'll be lucky if we don't get kicked out of here. I can see it now, the manager will come to the table and announce in a nasally voice there will be no talking about big dicks in his restaurant."

She hooted in laughter once again before finally regaining control of herself. Then, as if nothing out of the ordinary had happened, she batted her eyelashes at him. "What? It really is big, sheesh."

"That's why we call him Big Phil." His announcement started another round of laughter and set the pace for the rest of their lunch.

Nearly an hour later Sebastian found himself driving Bailey back to his office. "Are we still on for tonight?"

She was in a playful mood, a naughty mood if the way she leaned across the center console to kiss his mouth and fondle the length of his cloth-covered erection were any indication.

"Where are we going?"

Sebastian tilted her face, angling it to deepen their kiss. "It's a surprise."

"I think I've told you before, I don't like surprises." When Bailey poked her lip out in a bratty pout, Sebastian nipped it.

"You'll like this one, sweetheart. Promise." Sebastian let her go, missing her taste immediately. He climbed from his car then walked around to open the passenger door for her. It only took a minute to get to the door of her car.

"Why don't you follow me home?" The words came out in a husky little purr nearly unmanning him.

"No can do. If I do that, we won't make it back out until tomorrow and then you'd miss your surprise. We can't have that." Sebastian kissed the tip of her nose and left. It took everything in him not to take her up on her offer.

* * * * *

Bailey eyed Cat's front door with trepidation. This was the last place she had been expecting Sebastian to bring her tonight. She wasn't unhappy with his choice of eating establishments but Bailey had been hoping his surprise involved just the two of them.

"If my surprise is more group sex, I'm going to kill you," she warned somewhat teasing as she rang the doorbell.

"I was saving group sex for your birthday." His dry tone made her laugh. Leave it to Sebastian to say the unexpected.

"Wow, group sex, just what I wanted."

Clearing his throat nervously, Sebastian pulled her back into his embrace, resting his chin on her shoulder. "Maybe you should stop saying that?"

"What, group sex?" Bailey leaned to the side so she could see his face but not leave his arms. She never would have thought he would be shy about what they did. Hell, even she wasn't bothered about their little interlude anymore. "Why, are you embarrassed?"

"No, but you will be."

Yeah right. "Please, do I look like someone who gets embarrassed by a little group sex?"

"Bay…" his tone was warning but Bailey forged on, intent on razzing him.

"Group sex. Group sex." The front door opened up behind her as she sung in a high-pitch tone. "Group sex. Group sex."

Her teasing words were drowned out by a mild cry of "Surprise". It had her whipping forward, her hand over her pounding chest. Instead of Mason or Cat answering the door as she had been expecting, there was a hallway full of people who were staring at her in shock.

Their good-natured cheer trailed off, echoing like a dull roar in her head. The silence to greet her was louder than a sonic bomb.

"Surprise," Cat said weakly, her face flushed a deep red, and with good reason. Everyone was staring at Bailey and Sebastian and there was no doubt in her mind her words had been overheard.

Surprise was an official understatement. "Oh my God!"

Sebastian's deep chuckle from behind her didn't help matters at all. "I warned you."

Spinning back around to face him, Bailey punched Sebastian on the arm. It was either hit him or combust from the heat flushing her body. She was mortified and it was all his fault. He could have warned her. To think, he called her brat. "Try harder next time. I'm so embarrassed."

"I thought you didn't get embarrassed."

"Shut up." She stuck her tongue out at him before turning back around and smiling sheepishly at the group. "I totally knew you guys were there."

"Yeah right," called out Cat's older brother Ian, who was leaning against the wall with a beer. "Group sex, huh, I think this party is going to be a lot more fun than I thought."

His witty words broke the ice as everyone chuckled and Bailey, with a little prodding from Sebastian, stepped all the way into the house.

Laughing at her blunder, Cat pulled Bailey into the house and into the warmth of her arms. Cat hugged her as Bailey buried her head in her best friend's shoulders in shame. "I'm going to kill you," she whispered. "Ian is never going to let me forget this, is he?"

"Not a chance. Congratulations, woman. I'm so proud of you."

"Thank you. Thank you. I deserve this party and so much more." Bailey primped, posing with a hand on her hip, causing Cat to laugh as intended. "I can't believe you guys did this."

"Well, I would love to take the credit for it all but Sebastian was the ringleader behind all of this."

Bailey turned to look for the man in question and smiled when she saw him across the room talking to Mason. As if feeling her stare, he looked over at her and smiled in his special way that Bailey loved. Her heart seemed to pick up a salsa beat for a few seconds before returning to its regular rhythm. She was going to have to thank him later, much later, with a lot of enthusiasm.

Cat's knowing snort drew Bailey's attention back to her friend. "What?"

"I don't think you're as immune to him as you'd like to think you are."

"I have no idea what you're talking about." Cat's words had startled Bailey but she refused to let her know.

"Sure you don't, Bay. Just keep telling yourself that." Cat winked at her before walking away, leaving Bailey staring in her wake, shaking her head after her. Cat always had to have the last word.

Bailey didn't have time to dwell on her parting words though, because as soon as Cat left another well-wisher took her place. Hours passed before Bailey realized she hadn't had a minute of peace and quiet to herself.

She had been hugged, congratulated and teased unmercifully and she loved every second of it. Her favorite part of the evening though, was when Cat's brothers cornered her. Just talking to them for a couple of minutes made her feel homesick.

Bailey hadn't seen them in a while, even though she and Cat lived only an hour away from the city they'd grown up in. Although home for her wasn't the same residence since her mother had left husband number three and moved up north, but it was still where Cat's family lived and as far as Bailey was concerned, they were family enough.

Even though she was an only child, Bailey had never felt like one thanks to Cat's older brothers. The Vaughns were a large, boisterous, loving family Bailey loved as much as she loved her own. Larger than life, all three brothers were raven-haired, blue-eyed, drop-dead gorgeous men who proudly boasted of their machismo ways. They were the brothers she never had and they took great pleasure in teasing her as they would any sibling.

By the time she escaped them, her ass was sore from the spanking Garrett and Seth insisted she needed for not calling them and her cheeks hurt from laughing so hard. Their spanking was nowhere as exciting as the ones Sebastian was fond of giving her, but it still smarted just the same.

Her tingling rear reminded her she hadn't seen Sebastian in a while. Although she was having a good time, Bailey was tired and ready to go home, especially if it meant Sebastian and she could have a little one-on-one time to do some celebrating of their own.

On her way to find Sebastian, Bailey passed Big Phil, who was with a different woman than he had been with this afternoon. From the lazy look in their eyes, Bailey was sure they had been partaking of one of Mason and Cat's many rooms.

Not a bad idea.

"Have you seen Sebastian?" she asked as they stopped in front of her.

"Yeah," Phil offered, gesturing to the back of the house. "He was heading out onto the patio."

Offering thanks, Bailey heading toward the patio, grinning to herself as she heard the woman give a high-pitched giggle.

Big Phil indeed.

The slight chill in the air did little to cool Sebastian down. Sneaking outside went against everything in him but it was the only option he had unless starting a fight counted. And if there was anything Sebastian was sure of, it was fighting at Bailey's celebration party would be equivalent to stirring up a hornet's nest—while naked.

It hadn't taken him long to get tired of watching Bailey flit from man to man. Her smile was always bright and her arms always outstretched for a hug. If he had to watch one more minute of her hugging on Ian or being swatted by Garrett and Seth, things were going to get real ugly, real quick.

"There you are." Her voice wafted around him, light and airy, just like the breeze.

Sebastian turned around to face her. He forced his lips to curve in what he hoped was the semblance of a smile. "Yep, here I am."

Bailey stopped in front of him, her smile not as bright as before yet not completely gone. She tilted her head to the side, studying him. "Uh-oh, what's wrong?"

Not used to insane feelings of jealousy, Sebastian pulled her into his arms. There was no way in hell he was going to admit he'd been out on the patio sulking, throwing the equivalent of a tantrum.

"Not a thing, Bay, not a thing."

Without giving Bailey a chance to answer or even lean far enough away to look at him, Sebastian settled his mouth over hers. Her lips tasted of wine, sweet and fruity. It was impossible to pull away once he'd tasted her, leaving him no choice but to deepen the kiss, taking it to a whole new level.

Bailey shivered when his tongue swept into her mouth. The intimate caress left him breathless with need. With lips melded together, they vied for more, to get impossibly closer to one another while remaining in an upright position with their clothes on.

"Damn! You two are gonna burn down the place."

"Fuck!" Sebastian cursed. Seeing Ian drool over his woman was not something he was willing to deal with.

Bailey licked her lips, making his cock throb painfully against the cotton of his boxer briefs. When she peeked over his shoulder and giggled, Sebastian thought he would lose what was left of his patience.

"Was there something you needed, Ian?" Bailey's voice was soft as was the look she bestowed upon Ian, the man Sebastian was sure he had every reason to despise.

"Yeah, something so important it couldn't possibly have waited?" Sebastian sneered. He was angry, angry and jealous as hell. Not a good combination.

"'Bastian!" Bailey then turned toward the man who had so rudely interrupted them. "We'll be in in a few minutes, Ian."

There was an unholy smile curving the giant's lips as he turned to leave. If Ian were anything like Sebastian, the man was keenly aware of how much his presence, his closeness to Bailey, bothered him and was going to play on the weakness he'd so easily found in Sebastian.

It was the exact same thing Sebastian himself would do under the circumstances.

Bailey turned back to face Sebastian, her hands perched on her hips. The way she tapped her toe warned just how irritated she was and if he was in any way unsure of her mood, her words easily cleared up possible misconceptions.

"You weren't very nice to Ian."

Sebastian growled low in his throat. "I'm not in a nice mood. There's just something about three giant men hugging and spanking on my woman that pisses me off."

Sebastian stood rooted to the spot when Bailey advanced on him. He was probably putting his life in jeopardy by doing so. If the look on her face were any indication, Bailey wasn't particularly happy about his declaration. Sebastian wasn't sure whether it was the macho jealousy issue or the fact he'd declared she belonged to him and at this point in time, he didn't care.

"Let's not do this now, please. It's supposed to be a celebration, my celebration, so don't you dare ruin it by acting like an asshole!"

Oh yeah, she was pissed. She was also right. Sebastian had no right to ruin her night. And if she stayed away from the Vaughn brothers, she might very well get off without a spanking. Damn, he almost hoped she'd manage to get herself into some sort of trouble before they called it a night.

"Okay, sweetheart." Sebastian pulled Bailey back into his arms. "You win this round, but unless you want your ass heated by the flat of my hand, you'll behave yourself."

Her body became poker stiff against his. Sebastian had a hard time not laughing out loud when Bailey stomped her foot and flounced away.

That was his brat.

* * * * *

It seemed as if the party lasted forever. Sebastian had been as patient as possible but the evening had quickly worn thin on him. Of course, the anticipation of getting Bailey home and back in his arms might have had something to do with it.

She'd spent the rest of the evening in a snit, but aimed only toward him. To everyone else, she'd been all hugs and smiles. It was the hugging part that had her in trouble. She'd taken his words as a challenge, not the warning they were, and had spent the rest of the party shamelessly flirting and giggling with Catarena's three giant-sized brothers.

Bailey's insistence they were just friends had only made matters worse and soon Sebastian's last nerve was wound so tight he was sure it would snap with the slightest provocation. And here she was, sound asleep in the passenger seat of his car, oblivious.

"We're home." Sebastian gave Bailey's shoulder a little shake after pulling the car to a stop.

It only took a few minutes before they were comfortably ensconced in his living room. Bailey was wide awake and eyeing him warily from her seat on the couch. She kept her gaze trained on him as he removed first his tie and then his coat. When Sebastian reached for the top button of his shirt, she licked her lips. She was so damned beautiful she made him ache.

"Listen, 'Bastian, about tonight." There was a slight tremor to her voice as Sebastian continued removing his shirt. When he slid the belt from the loops of his trousers, she swallowed.

The action made her throat move in a way that reminded Sebastian of her going down on him. Hell! Just thinking about her hot little mouth wrapped tightly around his cock, sucking and licking, almost had him creaming his pants like a callow youth.

"Yes, about tonight. I owe you an apology for acting like the jealous jerk I am." Her eyes grew so wide Sebastian almost felt bad for getting her hopes up.

"So you're not mad then? Oh good!" she barreled on. "I was pissed about what you said…"

Bailey let her explanation trail off. But it was okay, Sebastian didn't need to hear any more. He knew exactly what had gone through the little brat's mind.

"Nope, I'm not mad. I'd never lay a hand on you when angry."

Her eyes narrowed a bit as if she were trying to figure out what he meant. It wasn't long before her luscious lips formed an O and her eyes grew wide once again. Sebastian stood before Bailey, nude from the waist up. He was looking over her head, scanning the room when she finally spoke.

"What…umm, are you doing?"

Sebastian looked down to where she sat on the couch and fought to keep his face straight, his tone stern. "I'm trying to make up my mind in what position I want you in when I spank you."

This time she stood. "Yeah, I don't think that's going to happen."

With narrowed eyes, Sebastian pinned her to the spot. "I haven't heard you say your safe word, Bay. You do remember it, don't you?"

"Yes."

"Let me hear you say it once just for practice, sweetheart. I don't want to go into this punishment with any doubts."

"Buddy! There, are you satisfied?" Bailey all but stomped her foot.

"Good. Real good. Now turn around and place your palms on the arm of the couch." Sebastian waited a couple of seconds before adding, "Unless you'd prefer to use your safe word?"

From the look on her face, Bailey took what he said as a challenge. With her chin tilted at a defiant angle, she whirled around until she was facing the couch. She gave her hips a naughty little swish and leaned into the correct position.

When Sebastian made no move toward her, she looked over her shoulder. "Did you want me to raise my dress for you?"

The damned vixen was going to be the death of him. Her sassy smile and wicked curves were going to do him in. Sebastian knew if he weren't careful, he could very easily end up wrapped even further around her little finger.

"That's okay, sweetheart, I think I can handle that part all by myself."

Chapter Seven

೮ა

It was official. Sebastian had straight up lost his mind. More than just his mind in fact, if he really thought she was going to hold still and let him spank her ass. Bailey couldn't even count the many ways it so wasn't going to happen.

Biding her time, she waited until she felt him approach from behind her before she tossed a glance over her shoulder at him, making sure she didn't move from her seductive pose. If she knew him as she thought she did, Bailey was sure the passive way she was leaning was turning him on. Sebastian had proven on more than one occasion he liked to be in charge.

"Just so there's no misunderstanding," Bailey raised a brow haughtily at him. "What exactly am I getting a spanking for?"

Sebastian matched her cavalier stare with one of his own. "Do you want me to say the list in alphabetical or numerical order?"

"Whatever floats your boat." Sebastian's hand flew back in the air and Bailey's body tensed waiting for the smack she knew would surely follow. But to her surprise, instead of making good on his spanking promise, he brought his hand down quickly, stopping it a mere breath away from her cheeks.

The bastard even had the nerve to chuckle at the way her breath caught in her throat, further angering her. He needed to be put in his place and fast.

"Well, we already know what floats my boat, don't we, doll?" Sebastian followed his words by bringing his hand to her rear and slowly raising her dress until it pooled in the middle of her back.

"Don't call me that!" Bailey bit out furiously. She tried to rise from the couch but was stopped cold by Sebastian, who pressed firmly on her back, keeping her in the position he'd ordered her to take.

"What…doll?"

"Yes."

Sebastian chuckled as he caressed her exposed cheeks lovingly. "Aren't you my doll baby?"

He said it in such a high-mannered way Bailey seriously doubted doll baby was a term of endearment. "Can't you remember my name?" she hissed. "Or do I have to work harder to make sure you scream it later?"

"I think you're confused, doll." Sebastian brought his palm down firmly on her upturned bottom. The sharp sting startled Bailey, who tried unsuccessfully to move from under his hand. "You're the one who will be screaming my name."

"In your dreams." *Smack! Whack!* "I'm going to kill you."

Sebastian chuckled, his disbelief evident in his laugh. "If you want me to stop, you know what to say."

"Bastard!"

"That's a B word, but not the correct one." Sebastian cracked his hand against the fleshy part of her bottom again, making her sensitive skin sting and tingle. He countered the smack with a tender rub that only made her ass burn all the more.

Her ass wasn't the only thing on fire though. Bailey would have never believed it in a million years but his little punishment was actually turning her on. Her clit was swollen and rubbing against the tapered cloth of her thongs, which was becoming increasingly damp by the second.

Her skin sizzled at his touch. A soft whimper escaped from her parched lips as Sebastian brought his hand down again for another stimulating blow.

"You're evil."

"And you're spoiled," he replied dryly.

How the hell was she so affected by what Sebastian was doing and yet he seemed as cool as could be? He was toying with her. "Get used to it because I'm not going to change."

"Neither am I. Do you see the quandary there?"

"Then I guess we'll just have to see who'll break first." It was a bit hard talking smack while getting a spanking but Bailey didn't know how to back down any more than he did.

Sebastian rained another smack on her rear, this time lower and softer than the previous ones.

His aim was dead on, spanking her clit with the teasing blow. "A challenge, huh? I accept."

The shock from his smack had her arching away from his touch. Her movement earned her another hit and a warning tsk from her sexual punisher. "Don't move again."

He had to be kidding. Not move, why didn't he just ask her not to breathe? "I'm going to…"

"I know, kill me, but not before I finish doling out your punishment."

"This so-called punishment is as insane as you. I did nothing wrong." Bailey didn't believe herself and neither did Sebastian, who responded in kind.

Whack!

His blow landed on her buttocks again. "Yes, because it's perfectly acceptable for you to allow those bastards to touch what's mine."

"Nothing on me is yours."

"That's where you're wrong." *Smack!* "Everything on you is mine and you damn well know it."

Never, Bailey screamed in her mind but not aloud. She wasn't crazy. Sebastian would take her word as a challenge and force her to admit something she wasn't ready to admit to herself.

When she didn't reply, Sebastian moved his touch back to her aching cream-coated clit, caressing her through her soaked covering. Bailey waited for the chuckle she was sure would follow, but much to her surprise and infinite relief, he said nothing. He was too busy ripping the last barrier between her sopping cunt and his hand away. The sound of the material being torn from her body had her shivering with anticipation. Finally he would give her what she craved. What they both craved.

"So pretty." His whispered words were like a caress in the dark. "So pretty and wet for me. Only me."

"Yes," Bailey replied, knowing instinctively what he wanted. Sebastian was as possessive as a dog with a bone and he would never share. Instead of frightening her, his caveman ways turned her on even more. It was official, she was a dirty little girl.

"You were trying to make me jealous tonight, weren't you?"

"No," she lied, gasping when he met her lie with a smack on her ass.

"Let's try this again." Sebastian moved his hand to her clit, pinching the aroused tip between his fingers, adding pressure and pleasure to her aching body. "You were trying to make me jealous tonight, weren't you?"

"Yes." The word was a gasp on her lips.

She closed her eyes as she whimpered his name. Son of a bitch, she was so close to coming. And she needed to. Bailey needed to come more than she needed her next breath. "Please, 'Bastian."

"Do you want to come?"

"You know I do."

"Then tell me," he ordered, and for the first time the need for more was evident in his voice. Maybe she wasn't the only one affected after all. "Tell me who you belong to."

"I belong…"

"Yes." Sebastian released his grip on her back and slid his hand underneath her body to her aching nipples. Tugging on the hard buds as he slipped his other fingers away from her clit and into her tight, moist sheath.

"I belong to you." Her declaration felt as if it had been dragged from deep inside her, but it was worth it. It was worth everything if it meant Sebastian would continue pleasuring her.

"And don't you ever forget it." Instead of being pleased by her admission, Sebastian seemed hell-bent on punishing her with pleasure. He thrust his fingers inside her, continuously driving her wilder and higher with each plunge.

Moaning and pleading for more, Bailey pumped herself back onto his probing fingers, her body begging for deep, harder penetration. She'd never felt so needy or aroused in her life. Her body cried out for more and Sebastian didn't disappoint her. He kept at her, teasing her, fucking her with his fingers, until she thought she would go mad.

Bailey felt herself spiraling closer to orgasm with each thrust of his nimble fingers and just when she thought she couldn't take another second of his mind-numbing finger-fucking, she came, screaming his name as the pleasure washed over her.

Sebastian was almost afraid he was having a wet dream and would awake before he got to finish it. The feel of Bailey wrapped so snugly around his fingers was erotic as hell but fingering her wasn't nearly enough.

He wanted her to come and then come again and again and again until she was hoarse from screaming his name, until her knees were weak from sexual exhaustion and she couldn't carry her own weight. That way she couldn't run and hide when she realized just how deep into a true relationship they really were.

Sebastian waited until Bailey's body relaxed before pulling his fingers from her drenched folds. He wasn't about to let her off the hook so easily though. With the impatience of a horny teenager, Sebastian dropped to his knees behind her.

With a hand on each ass cheek, he parted her for the flick of his tongue and held her exactly where he wanted her.

"Oh fuck! 'Bastian." Bailey's moan of delight wafted around them as did her sexy-as-hell scent.

Using the full length of his tongue, Sebastian licked her. She was salty sweet and so hot he thought she would burn him alive. He was hell-bent on feeling her come against his mouth and wanted to be sure Bailey knew it.

"Mmm, you taste good, Bay." Sebastian released her with one hand, using it instead to reach between her legs. He circled the hard little nub of her clit, eliciting a groan of submission from her.

When she moved her hips back, Sebastian thrust his tongue deeper into her tasty channel while finally rolling her clit between his fingers, applying just enough pressure to keep her perched on the edge yet not quite enough to send her over.

Sebastian lifted his face from between her thighs. "Fuck my face, sweetheart. Show me how much you like me tonguing your pretty little pussy."

His words seemed to drive Bailey crazy with need. In wild abandon, she did as he asked, thrusting her hips back at him, fucking his face, giving him even more of her sticky sweetness.

She was close, so close Sebastian could feel her muscles tighten beneath the hand he still had resting on her ass. Wanting to slow Bailey down, to give her building orgasm a little extra kick, Sebastian stopped fucking her with his tongue and instead changed to slow, languid strokes.

He licked and sucked the engorged lips of her cunt while holding her clit prisoner between his fingers. The need to see her explode, to taste everything she had to offer caused Sebastian to dip a finger into her hot box, coating it with her juices before trailing it up to the rosebud of her anus.

Her breath hitched before picking back up at a rapid pace. "I…uh. Oh God!" Bailey's words came out on a garbled moan as Sebastian sank knuckle-deep into the ultra-tight depths of her ass.

Her body tightened around his finger, making it impossible to thrust deeper. Sebastian was dying to get his cock inside of her but first he'd see her fully satisfied in every possible way.

"Relax, sweetheart. Open up and let me in while I lick you until you come. Be nasty with me, Bay. Let me love you my way."

Sebastian went back to work on her pussy, tasting and teasing until her body responded to the invasion of his finger, allowing him to move deeper with each thrust. What must have been overwhelming sensations tore a keening cry from Bailey's lips as her body tightened around him, against him, for him. Sebastian lapped everything she gave and demanded more, loving every minute of her body's submission to him.

There was no waiting. Sebastian had to have her now. He needed to feel her body respond to the driving thrusts of his cock buried deep within her while he fondled her breasts until their aching peaks were sensitive to his every touch.

Without waiting for Bailey to catch her breath, Sebastian slid his finger from the tight confines of her body. He then lifted her off her feet and made his way to the privacy of his bedroom where he proceeded to remove every stitch of their clothing.

Gloriously nude, Bailey lay sprawled across his sheets, her body his for the taking. "One of these days I'm going to take you slow and sweet, doll, but tonight isn't it."

Bailey lifted her arms over her head and held onto the intricate bars of his headboard. She looked spectacular, a sacrifice for his pleasure and his pleasure alone.

"I don't want slow and deep." Her voice was a hushed whisper. "Slow and deep would kill me." Bailey's voice grew stronger, her body more tense. "Just as I'm going to kill you if you don't get over here and fuck me."

Sebastian, who had climbed onto the bed and now lay beside Bailey, chuckled against her neck.

"Is that so?" He ran the fingers of one hand up the inside of her leg until he reached her heated core. Sebastian couldn't help but tease her, to revel in the way her body undulated at his every touch, wordlessly begging for another climax.

"If you don't want it slow and sweet, how do you want it?"

He already knew. The way her body moved in reaction to his touch made it evident. "Hard," she panted the word out as Sebastian sank two fingers into her pussy as deep as they would go. "And deep. Now, 'Bastian. Now!" She insisted when he kept stroking her from within.

Knowing her body was slick and ready for him, along with her command to be taken, were all the incentive Sebastian needed. In a matter of seconds, he'd sheathed his cock and then he was on her and in her. Bailey's body welcomed him, eagerly taking every inch of his rock-hard cock.

Sebastian knew he wouldn't last long. After feeling her pulse around his fingers and tasting her essence, he was ready to explode. Bailey hung onto the headboard and met him stroke for stroke with her hips, elevating herself in order to take his hammering thrusts deep.

When his orgasm hit, it hit hard and fast. Sebastian struggled through the mind-numbing sensations coursing through his body until he knew for sure Bailey had also found her release. When his pulse finally slowed enough to catch his breath, Sebastian levered his body off Bailey's. He left her long enough to dispose of the condom then climbed back into bed behind her. He pulled her back to his front, spooning her, loving the way she felt against him.

The feel of her body, all soft and pliant against his, only reminded Sebastian he was leaving for a few days on a business trip and how much he would miss Bailey. Unless he took her with him.

The idea hit nearly as hard and fast as his orgasm had. The mere thought of waking up to her in his arms brought a smile to Sebastian's face.

"Bay?"

"Hmmm?" Her sleepily grumbled answer made him chuckle.

Sebastian was already planning the short trip in his mind. They wouldn't have a whole lot of time, but there were so many things he wanted to take her to see, to do.

"I've got to go to San Antonio for a few days and I want you to go with me." Sebastian tried to ignore the way her body stiffened against him. "We can see the sights, sweetheart. Do anything you want."

She didn't even give his idea any thought before sitting up. Shaking her head, she said, "I can't, 'Bastian."

He tried not to feel angry at her denial but the feeling swept over him like wildfire burning through dense brush anyway. If she went back to their "friends with benefits" status after what they'd just shared, there were going to be problems.

"It'll be fun, Bay."

Her face was tense, the space between her brow furrowed as she sat on his bed, his sheet held over her breasts, hiding them from his gaze. Something about her covering herself made Sebastian want to lash out. Before thinking about the repercussion of his actions, he yanked the sheet from her hold, pulling it, as well as the rest of the covers, off the foot of the bed until she sat there before him as nude as the day she was born.

Bailey's eyes narrowed in anger. "I can't go because I have to work."

"So take a couple of days off."

The next thing Sebastian knew, Bailey was off the bed and scrambling for her clothes. "I haven't been there long enough to take days off for the sole purpose of fucking around, Sebastian. I don't have any sick or vacation days saved up."

His full name on her lips sounded more like a curse. If it were the money she was worried about, he could alleviate her worry with no problem. "It's not a problem, sweetheart. It's my treat and I'll compensate you for the days you miss if it's the money you're worried about."

Sebastian wasn't at all sure what he'd said to piss her off but if the way she stomped her way to the door and slammed out of it gave any indication to the extent of her anger, he was in deep shit and had just royally fucked up somehow.

*   *   *   *   *

BlackCat: He didn't say that.

Finally, someone was on her side. Bailey wanted to throw her hands in the air in relief. She didn't though, but only because she didn't want to look like a big idiot to the worker bees still hanging out in the office on their lunch break. Instead, Bailey pulled her chair closer to her desk and began to type in a frenzy.

MsThang: Yes he did. Compensate. COMPENSATE!!!!

If there were a way for her to have the words ring out across the line, she would have. Just typing the word made her angry all over again.

MsThang: As if my fucking time can be bought.

BlackCat: Bay, I'm sure he didn't mean it like that.

Startled at Cat's quick change of heart, Bailey made a "what the fuck" face at the screen. It took everything in her power not to pound her next comment into her keyboard.

MsThang: But he said it like that.

BlackCat: Girl, you should know by now with men it's not what they say, it's what they mean.

MsThang: I'm not a fucking psychic, Cat. I can't read his mind.

BlackCat: I have to say I'm really surprised he said it. Normally Sebastian is a bit more…ummm…smooth.

Bailey snorted. Any other day, she would have agreed in a flash, but right now, smooth was the last word she associated with the insensitive jerk.

BlackCat: So what did you do?

MsThang: I politely told him no thanks, dressed and asked him to take me home.

BlackCat: Politely?

MsThang: Yes, although it took everything inside of me not to rant and rave. I swear, sometimes I just want to beat his head in until the pink meat shows.

BlackCat: And the other times?

MsThang: The other times…

Biting down on her bottom lip, Bailey didn't know quite how to answer the question. She tapped her fingers on the keyboard, willing them to come up with an answer both she and Cat would believe. It was one thing to lie to herself, but to lie to Cat was a sin in itself, and besides, she wouldn't believe Bailey anyhow. One of life's cruelties was the ability best friends had to see through shit.

MsThang: The other times I don't.

BlackCat: Is that all I get?

Cat's question was followed by a raised brow smiley icon, which had Bailey smiling herself. She didn't think Cat would let her get away with her open-ended answer.

MsThang: When I work out my feelings, I promise you'll be one of the first to know.

BlackCat: I'll keep you to your word. Quick change of subject. I have a present for you.

MsThang: I like presents.

BlackCat: I just sent something to your email. Maybe it will help you work out your feelings just a tad.

Bailey seriously doubted it.

MsThang: Not unless it's an animated sledgehammer with a picture of Sebastian's head being bashed in over and over again.

BlackCat: LOL, close but no cigar. Check it out. I have to run. I'll talk to you later this evening.

Bailey had hardly typed in "bye" before her email beeped, informing her of incoming mail. Logging off the chat program, she quickly brought up her email, curious as to what Cat had been hinting at.

The second the email opened though, she wished Cat were there in front of her so she could slowly kill her. The last thing Bailey wanted to see while she was in a snit was a picture of Sebastian and herself at her celebration party. It was hard as hell to stay mad at him when she had to look in his pretty green eyes.

"Damn you, Cat," Bailey muttered under her breath. See if she took Cat's side next time she and Mason got into an argument.

In the picture, Sebastian had his hand around her shoulder and she was leaning into him. They looked so happy. She had been happy. Damn him.

The picture had been taken minutes before they left. She had teased and tortured Sebastian for most of the night, and she knew she was in for a world of trouble as soon as she left with him. From the predatory look in his eyes, he'd known too, two horny people looking forward to what the rest of the night entailed.

"Who's he?"

Bailey looked over her shoulder at Hillary, who was looking at the pictures on her desktop. "Not that it's any of your business, but it's a friend of mine."

Clicking on the apple in the corner, Bailey shut off her laptop, closing the top down even before the computer had completely closed out. Her private life was just that, private, and she had no intention of sharing it with anyone in the office, especially someone she couldn't stand. She was just going to let Hillary talk her smack and keep her peace.

Think Martin. Think Gandhi. Think you need this job, Bailey repeated over and over to herself.

"A friend, huh?" The unspoken challenge in the woman's words had Bailey gritting her teeth as she put her laptop in her carrying bag.

"Yes," she answered stiffly. Bailey knew if she didn't give some sort of reply to Hillary, the annoying woman would continue to pester her and Bailey wasn't in the mood.

"I don't blame you, girlfriend, I wouldn't claim him either. I mean if you're going to be sleeping with the enemy, you should at least make it someone worth getting lynched for, right?"

Bailey stood so quickly it startled Hillary, who stepped back as if in fear. So much for thinking Martin. "I'm not your friend, girl, and for your information my extremely handsome companion is more man than you'd ever be able to handle."

Hillary stopped retreating when it became clear everyone in the office was now watching them. "It looks as if you're handling him enough for the both of us."

"And loving every white inch of it." Bailey knew she should just walk away. It was the adult thing to do, the right thing to do, it just wasn't the Bailey thing to do.

"You're disgusting."

"Jealous much?"

Anger clouded the woman's dark face, showing a side of her Bailey had only imagined existed. "You think you're better than everyone else."

"Not everyone." Bailey gave Hillary a pointed look, letting the bitch know in no uncertain terms she wasn't one of the ones.

"You..."

"Ladies!" The booming voice of their supervisor Ray Cook cut off any further comment either woman might have made. Neither wanted to be the first to back down, but his presence could not be ignored. "I want to see both of you in my office now."

"Yes, sir." Bailey bit out. If she got fired because of this stupid bitch, she was going to kick her ass up and down the street. Life sucked butt. Only she could get in trouble on her lunch break.

* * * * *

Sebastian did his best not to scowl at those around him. He was in a black mood and it was all Bailey's fault. Last night, after their mind-numbing round of sex and an argument, over what Sebastian had no idea, she'd dressed then insisted he take her home. Other than that, Bailey hadn't said a word, not even when he'd walked her to her door.

There had been no goodnight kiss, no hugging or clinging. Hell, she hadn't even acknowledged his presence, much less acted as if she cared. Sebastian had spent part of the night tossing and turning. Her womanly scent had wafted around the room and clung to his sheets. It was nearly dawn when he finally gave up and went to the living room, intent on sleeping on the couch.

Sleeping on the couch hadn't worked either though. The minute he'd walked into the living room, his mind's eye had automatically pictured Bailey bent at the waist, her palms braced on the arm of the couch, luring him in with the sexy little shimmy of her hips.

"Mr. Emerzian? Would you agree, sir?"

Shit, shit, shit! Sebastian silently cursed himself. Here he was, in a business meeting, daydreaming about Bailey bent over his couch. His lack of attention could very well cause his client millions. As much as it pained him to do so, Sebastian had to look over his notes then ask the other man to repeat what he'd missed.

Business wise, the rest of the day went much better. Sebastian was on his mark and before the meeting adjourned, the idiot lawyer working against them, who thought he could win the case, was all but begging to settle.

His client accepted the settlement. All Sebastian had left to do in San Antonio was to see the paperwork was drawn up and signed by all included parties. He should be finished and able to return home first thing in the morning.

The thought of getting back to Bailey made him hard. Even knowing she was pissed off at him didn't lessen the magnitude of his arousal. He wasn't going to jump on the first flight home. No, Sebastian decided he'd stay out his visit. It would give Bailey some time to breathe, time to think. Of course, Sebastian wasn't sure whether giving her time was a good thing or not.

He would call her. Sebastian needed to hear Bailey's voice, even if it was cussing him out. After their conversation, he might even be able to sleep, something he'd not managed the night before.

Sebastian wondered if Bailey had also passed a sleepless night. She better have! He couldn't possibly be the only one in their relationship tumbling ass over end in love.

It was bad enough not to have a say in the matter of where his heart decided it belonged, but to do it with a prickly woman who was easily set off and only wanted to be his fuck buddy didn't seem fair.

Of course, not much in life was fair and Sebastian knew it. But he also knew Bailey had feelings for him whether she wanted to admit it or not. For the first time since she'd walked out the door last night, Sebastian smiled.

He had no time to feel sorry for himself. Bailey had dropped the gauntlet and although he'd wasted a bit of time, Sebastian was now deciding to take Bailey's actions as a clear challenge to him, to them. And for that she would pay in every sensually frustrating way he could think of.

Defying every impatient bone in his body, Sebastian waited until late, until he knew for sure Bailey would be home, to call her house. And when he did, all he got was a message telling him the number had been disconnected.

Sebastian hung up and tried again. When he got the same recording, he tried it a few more times. By the time he'd tried her number several different times and still got nothing, he grew extremely frustrated.

If she'd had her number changed in order to better avoid him, she was going to have one sore ass. Not knowing what else to do, Sebastian called Cat.

"'Lo?" Cat sounded groggy, as if she'd been asleep. Sebastian winced, knowing damned well if he'd interrupted her and Mason, Mason was going to fry his ass.

"Hi, Cat, it's Sebastian. Sorry to wake you." Only silence greeted him. "Cat? Are you there?"

"Huh?"

Oh yeah, she'd been asleep. "I can't get a hold of Bailey. Her phone says it's been disconnected."

This time muffled mumbles came over the line right before Sebastian heard Mason chuckle.

"Sebastian."

"Yeah, it's me. Tell Catarena I'm sorry I woke her."

Mason chuckled again, irritating the hell out of Sebastian. "What in the hell is so funny?"

Mason still sounded amused when he finally answered. "Cat's not mad you woke her. She's pissed because you hurt Bailey. Those two have got a code of honor between them. You should know better than to fuck with a pair, man."

Well hell. Sebastian rubbed a hand over the back of his neck, trying to ease the tension he felt there. He was also beginning to wonder whether or not he should catch the first flight out and not wait to work things out between Bailey and himself.

Work things out? Sebastian snorted, a sound having nothing to do with humor. He didn't even know why in the hell she was angry with him.

"I didn't call for a lecture, Mason. I called because I'm worried about Bay. Her phone's been disconnected."

"Her cell too?"

Sebastian could have kicked his own ass. Never once in the time they'd been…what? Sharing a bed? Pursuing a friendship? Had he thought to ask her for her cell phone number. What an ass he was. And from the sound of Mason's full-on laughter, the man was well aware he didn't have the number.

"If you could stop laughing long enough, I'd really appreciate the number."

"You know I'm risking life and limb by giving it to you." Mason's voice became dead serious. "Don't make me regret it, Sebastian. Do whatever you need to do to either smooth things over or end it."

Sebastian's hand tightened on the receiver. "I'm not giving her up, Mason. She's mine, just the same as Catarena is yours." He was completely adamant about the fact. Bailey could be pissed, she could argue and throw the biggest hissy fit known to man, but in the end, she would still belong to him.

In the split second it took for the thought to cross his mind, Sebastian made a decision. He was going to go home and set Bailey straight. She was going to explain to him exactly what he'd done that was so Goddamned horrible and then they were going to work it out.

He'd tie her naked to his bed if it was what it would take to get the brat to listen, but listen she would.

"Never mind, I don't need it. I'll be catching the first possible flight back home."

"Sebastian."

He chose to ignore the warning tone in Mason's voice. Instead, Sebastian concentrated on getting back home and what in the hell he was going to do to convince Bailey to give their relationship more than fuck-buddy status once he got there.

Chapter Eight

ะก

The loud pounding on Bailey's front door dragged her reluctantly from her bed. The last thing she was in the mood for was company after the day from hell she'd had at work yesterday but something about the persistent hammer warned her whoever was on the other side of the door wouldn't be so easily persuaded to go away.

All Bailey wanted to be was left alone. After being lectured to for almost an hour for her conduct at work, Bailey had slunk home, wanting nothing more than to bury herself under a mound of blankets and eat brownie fudge ice cream. To make matters worse, Sebastian was still out of town and he hadn't called once. This was definitely becoming the crappiest week of her life. And now there was a pounding jerk at the door.

A perfect ending to a perfectly awful week.

With a self-deprecating sigh, Bailey looked through the peephole, grimacing when she recognized the oblong face distorted through the eyehole. Just when she thought the day couldn't get worse, fate proved her wrong.

Bailey braced herself for the argument she knew would surely come and opened the door. "Mom. What are you doing?"

Faye Sanford pulled herself as straight up as her five-four frame would allow and shot Bailey a look that practically took her back in time, to a point in her life where her mother's every word was her command. "Is that the way you greet a guest?"

"Guest implies invitation," Bailey teased. "A visit from out of blue with you normally implies new husband."

"To think, the doctor said the drop on the head wouldn't affect you later on in life."

"What do doctors know?" They parroted at the same time, both grinning at their familiar repartee. Despite her initial grumble, Bailey was glad to see her mom. Fight as they may, there was a bond between the two of them no one could deny.

"So are you going to let me in?" Faye inquired as she pushed her way past her daughter.

Hurricane Faye was how Bailey always thought of her mother. She was a pint-sized version of Bailey. A whirlwind of beauty, she was constantly on the go and Faye had never met a stranger she didn't like. Unfortunately for the strangers, it was completely mutual and there was a trail of broken hearts littered across the country in her wake.

Bailey had grown up with more "uncles" than her grandmother had given birth to, and almost as many stepfathers as there had been Stooges. They had never stuck around long, but they had still somehow managed to make a life-long impression on her.

Beauty was as much of a curse as it was a blessing. It was a lesson Faye had taught her daughter first-hand.

"Make yourself at home." The sarcasm wasn't lost on her mother who dropped her oversized purse onto Bailey's table and did just that.

Propping her feet on Bailey's coffee table, Faye eased back on the sofa and wiggled until she found a comfortable spot. "So are you going to tell me what has you looking like you swallowed a pound of lemons or am I supposed to guess?"

"You're imagining things."

Faye raised a brow, a sarcastic look that had been passed from mother to child. "Guess it is."

"Mom." Bailey grumbled plopping next to her. "It's nothing. I'm just tired."

"Let's start with the obvious financial issues."

"No, everything is fine."

Faye snorted at Bailey's obvious lie. "I tried calling you this morning but the phone seems to be disconnected. How much do you need?"

"I don't need anything. Really. The phone company didn't disconnect my line. I did."

"Right."

"No, Mom, I did." Bailey knew her line of reason wouldn't make much sense to her mother, whose idea of fixing financial issues was to call her latest ex for an advance on her settlement. Bailey never wanted to be like her. She got herself in her money mess and she'd get herself out. Independence must have been a gene she inherited from her father, whoever he was. "I have a cell phone with more minutes than I'll ever use in a lifetime. It doesn't make sense to pay for two phones."

"That's ridiculous."

"No, Mom, wearing Juicy Couture at your age is ridiculous."

Faye swatted Bailey on the leg. "Bite your tongue, I could pass for your older sister."

"Sure you can," Bailey snickered. "My much, much, much, much older sister."

"Ungrateful is what you are. To think I flew all the way out here to give you your graduation present."

Bailey rolled her eyes. She wasn't buying it for a minute. "Sure you did."

"I did. I would have come to your party but I didn't get the invitation in time."

"It was kind of last minute."

A sly look came over Faye's pretty face. "No big deal wasn't the impression I got from your little party planner."

"Cat?" Bailey asked, confused.

"No, sweetie, I didn't speak with Cat."

"Who did you speak to?" *Don't say Sebastian. Don't say Sebastian.*

"A Sebastian, I believe."

Damn it. Loving Faye as she did, the last thing she wanted was for her to ever meet Sebastian. "Oh."

"Oh. Is that all you're going to say?"

Finally the reason for her mother's visit dawned bright and clear. "You didn't come here to give me a graduation present. You came here to pump me for information about my love life."

"Ah-ha." Faye pounced. "You two are involved."

Stupid. Stupid. Stupid. Why the hell did she say that? "No, Mom, we're just friends."

"The kind of friends who get naked though, right?"

"You know," Bailey frowned as she stood, "normal mothers and daughters don't talk about each other's sex lives."

Bailey headed to the kitchen to escape her mother's inquisition. If she were going to have to deal with her mom's crap this early in the morning, she was going to need a larger dose of caffeine. Unfortunately for her, Faye was fast on her heels.

"Since when have we ever been normal?"

"Never," Bailey grumbled.

Faye nodded her head happily. Crossing her arms over her abundant chest, she leaned against the sink next to Bailey. "All right then, tell me about him."

"There's nothing to tell. We're just friends."

"Please, you can't be just friends with a man. You're too damn beautiful."

That was just insulting. Sebastian didn't give a rat's ass how she looked and he was her friend, one of the best friends she'd ever had. "Sebastian doesn't see me as just a pretty face. He happens to like me for me, Ma. I know shocking as it is, we were just friends for a long time."

"But you're not just friends anymore, are you?"

Would she ever learn? "I wouldn't say 'just friends', but it's not as if we're dating or anything."

"Oh okay. Well, are you dating anyone?"

"No."

"Is there anyone you want to be dating?"

"No." Where was she going with this? The idea of going on dates with other guys no longer appealed to her, especially since Sebastian tended not to take it so well when she did.

"But you do see him and you like him."

"Of course I like him. He's a great guy. Funny, kind, he has such a big heart but an even bigger mouth. Stupid boy. I mean sometimes I just want to..." Making a choking motion with her hands, Bailey envisioned him in front of her, repeating, "I'll compensate you", over and over again. Sometimes he could be such a stupid jerk. He was her jerk but an insensitive one nevertheless.

"Oh Bay."

Her mother's words brought her out of her murdering fantasy. Looking over at Faye, Bailey was surprised by the look of joy on her mother's face. "What?"

Happy tears clouded Faye's chocolate eyes. Reaching for Bailey, she cupped her daughter's cheeks lovingly. "Don't you see? You're in love."

What the hell! "I'm not in love."

She was just envisioning his death by her own hands. That wasn't love. It was homicidal rage.

"Honey." Dabbing at the corner of her eyes, Faye chuckled. "Trust me, if there's one thing I know it's love, and you're knee-deep in it."

Bailey hoped her mother really didn't think she was the Don Juan of love. "Mom, you can't really believe you're some kind of expert on love."

"I surely do." Fayed narrowed her eyes at Bailey's burst of laughter. "Just because I suck at marriage, doesn't mean I suck at love. Although I do occasionally suck because of love."

"Ewww, Mom!" Bailey shuddered, not wanting to even think of her mother in a sexual way. "You're sharing way too much now."

"Don't be so silly. There's no such thing as sharing too much."

"So says you." Her mother gave head. Just one of the many things she could have gone her entire life not knowing.

"Go get dressed. We're going out."

"Why?"

"Because we're celebrating. It's not every day a woman's daughter—"

"Or a much, much older sister—"

"Falls in love." Faye finished with narrowed eyes. "Don't contradict me, girl. Go. Now."

"Fine," Bailey grumbled, intent on getting the last word, "but it's not love…"

"If you say so." Although Faye was saying the right words, Bailey was sure she didn't mean them.

She really should have just stayed in bed.

* * * * *

Sebastian crawled wearily from his bed. He ran a hand over his face then scratched his chest. The stress of the past few days compounded by the late night flight he'd finally managed to reserve a seat for had worn him out.

Padding barefoot to the bathroom, he took a quick shower and dressed for the day. Sebastian checked his watch before heading out the door. He had every intention of seeing Bailey. He was going to go by her apartment and talk to her if he had to tie her to a chair to accomplish the task.

Just thinking about Bailey tied and at his mercy did all sorts of things to his body. Sebastian adjusted the front of his trousers, allowing his hardening cock more room. It still amazed him how little control he had over his raging hormones where Bailey was concerned.

Sebastian pulled his car to a stop in front of Bailey's apartment. Looking forward to seeing her, even if he knew they would argue, he moved at a fast pace toward her apartment.

He knocked on the door and waited. When nothing happened, he pulled out his cell phone and called her, listening with his ear to the door. There was no phone ringing from within her apartment and he once again got a recording telling him her number had been disconnected.

"Bailey," Sebastian shouted as he once again knocked on the door.

There was still no answer or even a sound of movement. Sebastian pounded on the door, hoping maybe Bailey was still asleep and his pounding would wake her. He was just doubling up his fist to pound again when a door down the breezeway opened.

From the frown marring the old woman's face, it was obvious Sebastian had woken her up. "Sorry," he grumbled, heading back to his car.

It was early but it wasn't that damned early. Evidently Bailey was already at work. But on a Saturday? For a minute, Sebastian thought about hunting her down at her job site but quickly changed his mind. It was the weekend, besides only as a last resort would he do something so drastic. He'd give her the day but tonight he was going to return to her place and camp out on her doorstep until she either came home or answered, and then he'd find out what the hell happened to her phone.

Sebastian had no sooner stepped through the door to his office when his private phone line rang.

"Emerzian."

"Finally made it in, did you?" Phil's voice boomed.

"Well if it isn't Big P." Sebastian had known the man for years but still loved to tease him relentlessly about his nickname.

"That's what all the pretty ladies tell me." Phil was cowboy from the top of his hat to the tips of his boots. And if his appearance didn't convince a person, his Texas accent sure the hell would.

"How did the meeting in San Antonio go?"

Sebastian could hear the longing in Phil's voice. The man loved his home state and hoped to make the meeting himself but had had to back out at the last minute due to a court date he couldn't postpone.

"Good enough that I'm here to settle the paperwork on a Saturday. They settled. Signed, sealed and I'm delivering."

"Wooo wheee, you've got some fancy footwork going on in them loafers of yours, partner. I say we head over to The Boulevard for lunch and a drink to celebrate."

Sebastian chuckled. Phil could make a celebration out of just about any occasion. "I'll meet you over there."

After disconnecting, he gathered a few files to take home. Once on the road, the trip to the club took no time at all. Sebastian spotted Natalie's long, curly brown hair the minute he walked through the door.

She sat at a table, alone. She looked troubled as she thumbed through the pile of papers in front of her. When she spotted him though, she was all smiles.

"Hey, sexy."

Natalie looked as gorgeous as ever, even if the dark circles rimming her eyes told just how tired she was. The woman worked entirely too hard and had no one to take care of her as far as Sebastian knew.

He leaned over and gave her a chaste kiss on the cheek. "When you're ready to talk, I'll be here." Sebastian knew she was having problems with her bastard of an ex-husband, he just didn't know to what extent or even if it was what was worrying her.

"I will," she assured him. "I assume you're meeting with Big P. He's already at your table." Natalie shook her head as if bemused. "He's only been here for ten minutes and already has the attention of every female in the room who isn't already otherwise occupied creaming themselves. Simply fucking amazing."

Sebastian followed Natalie's gaze to the table she kept reserved for Phil and him, and sure enough, there sat Phil with a waitress all but swooning over him. He wasn't sure whether they were actually special patrons to her place or if it was just the amount of money they had a tendency to spend there that guaranteed them a table every time they stepped foot through the door.

"Guess I'd better go save him then." After giving Natalie's arm a gentle squeeze, he turned and walked away.

The room was pretty quiet, much more so than at night. Sebastian still wasn't convinced it was in Natalie's best interest to open for lunch but she hadn't asked his opinion so he hadn't given it. Sebastian might be her lawyer, but he wasn't her keeper. After hearing about her marriage, Sebastian doubted Natalie would ever allow a man control over her again. Neither physically nor emotionally.

Sebastian moved toward the table at his normal sedate pace. He smiled kindly to the huge, obviously fake-chested blonde waitress. "Scotch on the rocks, please." The woman scurried away, as fast as one could scurry wearing spiked heels, to get his drink.

"Now what did you go and do that for? I was enjoying her company."

Sebastian snickered. "I swear to God, Big P, either they have penis radar or you're paying for it."

Phil's gaze narrowed. He seemed genuinely affronted. "I've never had to pay for pussy."

At the same time Phil ground out the little tidbit of information, the waitress came back. She set his drink on a cocktail napkin in front of him, a giggle spilling from her ruby red lips. She brushed against Phil then set off to the next table.

"Glad to hear you get your fill of pussy for free."

Phil was looking behind Sebastian, staring would actually describe the intent look he was bestowing upon whomever was behind him.

"There's something going on with her."

Sebastian casually turned in his seat to see who Phil was talking about, only to come gaze to gaze with Natalie, who immediately looked away, as if she'd been caught doing something wrong.

"I haven't seen her smile in weeks."

Sebastian had noticed Natalie watching Phil in the past but he'd never witnessed any return of the attraction. Until now.

"And this bothers you because?" Sebastian raised a brow, a bit of challenge to his words. He knew Phil well, knew he wasn't the settling-down type. Hell, Phil wasn't even the screw-the-same-woman-for-more-than-a-week type.

"Because I like to see her smile."

With a resigned sigh, Sebastian said what was on his mind. "I know it's not any of my business but I think it's a bad idea."

There was no need to clarify just what he thought was a bad idea because Phil cut him off before he ever got the chance. "You're right. It isn't any of your business."

Sebastian gave Phil a sharp nod. He had more he wanted to say but decided against it. Phil being six feet three if he was an inch didn't have anything to do with it.

Phil might come across as a ruthless businessman more times than not but Natalie wasn't a pushover either. If Phil decided to pursue her in any way, shape or form, the fireworks were going to fly.

Sebastian and Phil enjoyed the rest of their lunch without too many distractions. He'd dropped the subject of Natalie although Sebastian caught him glancing her way more than once.

"I'll see you in the office Monday morning," Sebastian said when they parted ways. He spent the rest of the day shopping for a few adult items he hoped he'd have the chance to break in on Bailey.

By the time evening rolled around, Sebastian was so sexually frustrated and hard he couldn't think straight. He took a cold shower and had a good jerk session, hoping to ease some of the tension running through his body.

After dressing casually in khakis and a pullover shirt, he drove back to Bailey's. When he reached her door, he knocked, praying there wouldn't be a repeat of his morning fiasco. He was just lifting his hand to knock again, even louder, when the door opened.

"'Bastian." Her voice was husky and soft. The silk robe she wore clung to every curve of her luscious body and barely reached her thighs. Sebastian followed the hem up to the loosely tied sash at her waist and cursed. There was no way in hell he was leaving without sinking balls-deep in the hot sheath of her pussy first.

Bailey backed away as Sebastian took a step forward, invading her space. "Come here, Bay."

Bailey had to blink her eyes to make sure she wasn't dreaming. It was almost as if he had materialized from her fantasy, the very vivid fantasy she had been in the process of bringing to life before she had heard the knocking on her door.

When his lust-filled words penetrated her clouded mind, Bailey knew instantly he wasn't a figment of her very active imagination. He was here, and from the stormy look in his eyes and the bulge protruding from his pants, he was in the exact same mood she was in.

But Bailey wasn't going to let him off so easy. Sebastian had been gone two days and hadn't made a single attempt to contact her. For his offense, she should at least punish him by withholding sex for at least five minutes or so.

Yet, when she opened her mouth to blast him, Sebastian pushed her farther into the apartment and slammed the door shut behind him. He gazed at her, silently daring her to say something, but Bailey couldn't have spoken to save her life. There was an intensity radiating off him unlike anything she had ever seen before. It spoke volumes and chapter one clearly said, "I'm not in the mood to fuck around."

Bailey's nipples tightened immediately. She couldn't help it. Her body knew exactly what it wanted, even if she was too foolish to admit it to herself. "'Bastian."

"No." Sebastian moved quickly, his stride eating up the short distance between them. "No more fighting, Bay."

Before she knew what was happening, Sebastian bent forward and scooped her up, tossing her gently over his shoulder. Gasping, she grabbed hold of the tail of his shirt, surprised beyond belief. "What are you doing?"

"Taking you to the only place where you ever seem to listen to me." His words were followed by a quick smack to her upturned ass. Not the easy warm-up tap she was used to from him, but a sharp one that stung her and excited her all at the same time. Bailey squeezed her thighs together as her pussy began to moisten. Her ass felt inflamed yet Bailey wanted more.

"Don't fidget," he warned, giving her another smack for good measure.

Bailey dug her nails in his back in retaliation as she tried to calm her pounding pulse. "Then don't hit me."

His hand landed again as if she hadn't spoken.

"I should give you a spanking for opening the door wearing this in the first place," Sebastian growled as he slipped his hand underneath the short loose-fitting silk wrap.

When he touched her bare flesh, Sebastian stopped in his tracks. Flipping up the end of the robe, he softly rubbed his hand against her heated flesh. Before he could growl at her again though, his fingers slipped down her crease into her sopping wet cunt.

Bailey whimpered and tightened her grip on him as his fingers brushed against her erect, damp clit. "God, baby…" His words sounded as choked as she felt. Bailey tried to tighten her thighs again, ashamed at the way her body was responding to him, but Sebastian wasn't having any of it.

"Don't," he ordered softly. "Don't hide this from me. Ever. You're wet for me and I'm as hard as granite for you. This is how it will always be between us, Bay."

Sebastian continued to tease her sensitive bud as he talked, his words arousing her as much as his touch. How he managed to torment her and walk all at the same time was a mystery to Bailey, but by the time they were in her bedroom, she was no longer baffled, just grateful. She had to have him or she was going to combust.

Slipping his hand from between her legs, Sebastian leaned forward, depositing Bailey on her bed, legs spread wide.

When Bailey went to move back farther on the bed, Sebastian stopped her. "Did I give you permission to move?"

"I didn't know I needed it."

"Well, now you do." Sebastian took his glasses off and went to place them on her nightstand but stopped when he saw what was lying on top of the wooden table. He tossed her a teasing glance prior to picking up the toys she had been about to use before he'd rudely interrupted her. "It looks as if I came at just the right time."

"So says you." Bailey refused to blush or act coy. She was a woman with a very healthy sexual appetite and it was nothing to be ashamed of. "They've been the only company I've had for a while."

"They better have been," he warned. "But since I hate to disappoint a lady, I'll make sure they'll be well used tonight."

Sebastian dropped the toys next to her on the turned-down bed. Before Bailey could ask why she needed them now, he grabbed the hem of his shirt and pulled it over his head. Her mouth went dry instantly as he lowered his hands. Unbuckling and unzipping himself, Sebastian removed his pants, freeing his erect cock to her hungry gaze.

Toys, she didn't need any toys when she had him to play with.

"From the greedy look in your eyes, brat, I'd say your babies haven't been doing a good job of keeping you satisfied."

Bailey would have replied if he were lying, but he wasn't. Nothing filled her as he did. Anything else was a poor substitute for the real thing. When Sebastian dropped to his knees in front of her, Bailey could have cried her thanks to the heavens. And when he touched his lips to her soaked ones, she actually did.

Sebastian didn't stay gentle for long. His hand spread her legs farther apart as his tongue speared inside of her, drinking her cream directly from her hot center. He lapped at her cunt like a starved kitten, teasing her clit with long, hard strokes.

When she thought she'd go mad on pleasure, Sebastian brought his hand into the action, plunging two fingers into her dripping cunt, pumping his fingers inside of her until they were covered with her thick, sticky juices then drawing them slowly out and down to her rosette where he coated her tight, dark hole.

Bailey whimpered and dug her nails into the bedding, pushing down onto his probing fingers. She wanted Sebastian to fill her, in every hole and every way possible.

"Patience, baby," he ordered as he brought his fingers back to her cunt, soaking them again before dragging her warm juices back to her asshole.

This time he slipped a probing finger into her tight hole, lubricating Bailey with her own juices. He thrust his finger into her over and over again, stretching her, lubing her, readying her for the second finger he slipped in, filling her backside as she'd never been filled before.

"'Bastian." Bailey cried his name as he drank from her, his tongue spearing into her gripping pussy as he continued to thrust his fingers into her. Fire shot up her spine, bowing her back as she came in wave after wave of pleasure. Despite her ear-piercing scream of pleasure, Sebastian never stopped. He continued to pump inside of her with his fingers in one hole and his mouth at the other, and just when Bailey thought she couldn't take a second more, she came again, this time weakly crying his name.

She couldn't take any more, but she wanted more. She wanted him. "Fuck me," she pleaded. "Fuck me, 'Bastian."

Sebastian eased his mouth from between her legs and rose to his feet. He kept his fingers where they were though, slowing his thrust to lazy, long strokes. "Where?"

"Anywhere."

"Even here?" He punctuated his words with a deep thrust that made Bailey cry out with pleasure."

"Yes." Right now, Bailey didn't care where he fucked her as long as he did. "Just get inside of me."

"Yes, ma'am." Sebastian pulled his fingers slowly out of her. Moving quickly away from the bed to her dresser once more. He was back before Bailey had a chance to catch her breath. "This is going to be a little cold."

"This…what…God!" Bailey gasped as his cold finger penetrated her again. Apparently he'd found the lube she kept in her drawer. He worked her over quickly, the chill of the gel a distant memory as he added a second finger into her, scissoring them inside of her, stretching her so she could take his thick member.

Bailey cried out and dug her nails into the bedding when he added the third finger. Her body broke out in a fine sheen of sweat. She felt so tight and full, but before she could protest, he pulled his fingers from her, replacing them with the head of his cock.

"Push out, baby." He ordered hoarsely as he pressed forward. The slick bulb of his head pushed through her tight ring and into the depths of her warmth. "That's it, baby, open for me and swallow me whole."

"Oh…'Bastian." She was almost weeping from the pleasure. The pressure was so intense Bailey didn't think she'd ever be able to take him fully inside of her. Gripping the quilt, she held on for dear life as Sebastian pulled back slowly, drawing his cock almost all the way out then pressing forward again. Bailey gasped and closed her eyes as he slid to the hilt inside of her.

"God! You're so tight. So hot and tight for me." Sebastian shook with strain. His hands loosened their punishing grip on her hip and reached aimlessly next to her side. "From now on, I want you primed and ready for me to take you here at all times. This feels too damn good to be just a one-time thing."

Bailey couldn't agree more.

When Bailey heard the distinctive buzz of her vibrator, she opened her eyes and stared in surprise into his. Where the hell did he think she had room to put that right now? "I don't think…"

"Don't think, baby, just feel."

Bailey bit her lip and nodded, trusting Sebastian not to hurt her or at least not to hurt her in a bad way.

Sebastian turned the vibrator to high and touched it to her tender clit. If it weren't for him being lodged firmly in her ass, Bailey would have shot right off the bed. "Too much," she protested with a breathless cry, yet even as she urged him to move the toy away, her hands swiftly moved to her breasts so she could play with their beaded tips.

"I'll stop doing it the second you stop liking it." He lightened the vibrator's movements on her tortured clit as he began to gently pump into her ass.

"Bring your knees to your chest, Bay," he ordered her roughly, grasping her calves and moving her legs when she didn't hurry to obey him.

Bailey felt raw and exposed. The new position left her more open and vulnerable to his every desire, something Bailey was sure he had known would be in his favor.

"Your pussy is getting so wet for me. Leaking out your sexy cream, spilling it everywhere. You're a dirty girl now. And do you know what we do to dirty girls?"

Bailey knew exactly what he did to dirty girls. "Spank them."

"That's right, dirty baby girl. We spank them." Sebastian removed the vibrator from her tender clit and placed it at her beckoning, sopping wet opening. "Now take a deep breath, baby, and let Sebastian come out and play."

Bailey inhaled deeply, preparing herself for what she not only knew was going to happen but for what she wanted to happen. Thanks to Sebastian's desire, she didn't have long to wait.

After coating the length of the vibrator with Bailey's juices, Sebastian pulled it down and centered it at the mouth of her sex, plunging it deep into the recess of her tight hole. All the more tighter now since he was filling her from just a membrane below.

She was stuffed full of cocks. And Bailey loved every dirty inch of it.

"Fuck me. Fuck me," she cried out harshly, her hips jerking in response to the phallic toy Sebastian was now thrusting deep inside her. His hand moved over her cunt, stuffed to the brink with the vibrating cock, to her engorged clit, hard and aching to be pleased. He strummed her bud between his fingers as she powered herself down onto his thrusting cock.

Then surprisingly Sebastian did the one thing she hadn't been expecting. He spanked her clit. Not brutal smacks, but sharp taps over and over again as he fucked her. She moaned his name, begging for what, she wasn't sure.

"You're so fucking hot, baby." He rose to his knees on the bed, pulling her hips higher with him. Bailey was so used to seeing him in charge and in control, but right now, he looked far from in control. His face was a bundle of tormented desire as he slammed his hips harder against her, driving his cock so deep inside her she saw stars.

Bailey nearly screamed as lust consumed her. She writhed on the bed, lost in the power of her pleasure. Within seconds her body was shaking from the power of her climax. Colors flashed before her closed eyes and her chest rose harshly as she struggled for air. This had to be the most intense bout of sex she had ever had in her entire life.

Never in his life had Sebastian fucked or been fucked so intensely. The thought of never again holding Bailey in his arms made him panic. What they had done together in her bed had gone way past fucking. While not lovemaking in a traditional sense of the term, it was definitely more than sex.

Sebastian gave a silent snort of laughter at himself. He'd just been buried balls-deep in the hottest ass in the world, which belonged to the woman he planned to make his, and he was dissecting what they'd done as if it could be categorized.

He helped Bailey move farther on the bed before covering her. Once she was comfortable, he placed a kiss on her temple. Bailey's pulse still thumped wildly. The knowledge made Sebastian want to keep her just as she was, sated and overcome with sensual exhaustion, for the rest of their natural lives.

"Going?" Bailey's murmured question was whispered so low he barely heard her.

Her eyes remained closed, her face buried in the pillow beneath her head. The sheet didn't quite cover the swell of her ass. Just the sight of her sprawled across the bed as if she didn't have a care in the world and would remain there, waiting for him to return, brought Sebastian's cock springing back to life.

Sebastian made quick work of cleaning himself and returning back to the bed where he proceeded to clean Bailey with a warm washcloth before he scooped her body against his, her back to his front. He absolutely loved holding her and could picture them in the same position every morning for the rest of their lives.

His cock ached for the feel of her. Sebastian smiled at Bailey's lack of protest when he snuggled his cock between her thighs from behind. He did nothing to enter her. Just the feel of her warm flesh against his engorged length was enough.

Bailey squirmed in his arms just a bit before scooting away from his hold. Sebastian hoped like hell she wasn't going to start arguing with him to leave because there was no way in hell he was going to leave her.

It was probably best to just get it all out in the open and get her bratty blow up over and done with. "I'm not leaving you tonight, so you might as well forget it." Sebastian was willing to argue to the end, to all but overrule any objection she might have on the matter.

Bailey stopped on the edge of the bed and turned. She was sitting with her back to him and not a stitch of clothing to cover her. The delicate line of her spine beckoned to him, urged him to run his tongue down its length and start making love to her all over again.

The sassy smile curving her lips held no anger, nor did the devilish glint of her dancing brown eyes. "It's forgotten."

From the look on Bailey's face, she enjoyed keeping him off balance. "Brat."

This time, she did exactly as he expected. She stuck her tongue out at him. Sebastian could think of many things to do with her tongue. He'd have to list them for her. It surprised him she was in such a good mood, given the last time he had seen her she'd been livid.

He waited until she was once again between the sheets, in his arms. This time they were facing one another. Her leg was settled over his hip, the rigid length of his shaft nudging her heat, gaining only enough entrance to tease.

"I'm not sure what happened while I was gone to get you in such a good mood, sweetheart, but my vote is all for it."

Bailey stiffened in his arms as if his words had just reminded her she was supposed to be angry with him. When she placed her hands flat against his chest in preparation to push him away, Sebastian tightened his arms around her.

"Relax, Bay. We'll talk about it later. Right now, all I want to do is hold you and feel your body against mine." Sebastian snuggled her head closer. "Besides, I already told you I was staying and you agreed," he murmured the words against her hair.

Several minutes passed, minutes in which Bailey relaxed in his arms. She gave a sexy little sigh as her breathing deepened. There was still one question on Sebastian's mind, one he couldn't wait for morning to ask.

"I tried to call you while I was gone, Bay. Why did you have your number changed?"

She wiggled against him, seeking a more comfortable position. Her one-worded answer was spoken against the curve of his neck. "Didn't."

Sebastian chuckled. He'd worn her out with their lovemaking. It was something any man would be proud of. As much as he hated bothering her, she still hadn't answered the question to his liking.

"Then why isn't your phone working, baby?"

This time she made a mewling noise of irritation as she flung her arm over her head. "Cell only...too expensive...both." Her answer was muffled against his neck, her words a sleepy whisper, but Sebastian understood perfectly.

When Sebastian moved just enough to kiss her lightly, he was greeted by a cute little snore. He tightened his arms, pulling her closer. "Not anymore, Bay. You're mine and I take care of what's mine." His next words were spoken into the dark just before the darkness of sleep crept in. "I love you, Bailey Edwards."

* * * * *

When Sebastian woke the next morning, Bailey was already in the bath. Taking long baths was something she'd confessed early on in their relationship to loving. Seeing her there, sitting in the tub with suds covering her body, had him rock-hard in the blink of an eye.

"Damn, Bay, you should have woken me."

She smiled back at him. "I'm soaking because it's my 'me' time and because I'm sore after last night. Inviting you along would have defeated the purpose."

"Good sore or bad sore?" Sebastian had to know. Had he gone too far, pushed her body beyond what it could take?

Bailey must have recognized the look on his face. "Good sore, 'Bastian, so stop worrying."

He heaved a sigh of relief.

"Going somewhere?" Bailey motioned with a suds-covered hand to where he stood.

"I'm meeting Mason at the gym. Meet me at Mason and Catarena's later?"

Bailey arched a perfectly plucked brow at him. "For?"

"Mason and Catarena invited us over for lunch. I, uh…guess I forgot to mention it."

Bailey giggled. It was so good to see her in a lighthearted mood. "I'll see you there then."

Sebastian kissed Bailey lightly on the lips before leaving the bathroom. He dug into his wallet and pulled out enough money to cover the cost of having her phone reconnected. It wasn't safe for her not to have a phone. Cell phones were great but required batteries to be kept charged. Sebastian wasn't willing to take the chance something would happen and Bailey wouldn't be able to call for help if need be.

He quickly scrawled a short note letting Bailey know what the money was for. With a carefree whistle on his lips, he left her apartment thinking only of finally seeing her again at Mason and Catarena's house.

Chapter Nine

ॐ

There had been times in the last seven or so months since she'd known Sebastian that Bailey wanted to kill him. Today was the first time she wanted to kill, bring him back to life and then kill him all over again. No, killing him was too kind. She wanted to hurt him as he'd hurt her.

Casting her gaze from the busy street to the bundle of cash splayed across her passenger seat, Bailey felt her anger rising even higher. He had easily turned one of the best days in her life to one of the worst ones with a single note and a wad of cash left on her nightstand like some cheap trick. Bailey's heart broke in two when she read his note.

The two little sentences he had so carelessly scrawled across the back of an envelope were branded into her memory. *This should be enough money to turn your phone back on and a little extra to buy yourself something pretty. Gather the rest of your bills together and I'll write you a check.*

Bailey had left the note crumbled on her bedroom floor, right where he'd left her self-respect.

How dare he! And why on God's green earth did it always come back to money with him? Why couldn't he just be... The loud blaring of a car horn from behind her yanked her back from her rage.

Bailey had to concentrate. It would do no good to get herself killed before she had the chance to kill him.

As she skidded to a stop in front of Cat's house, Bailey spotted Mason and Sebastian in the driveway getting out of Mason's car. The smiling duo had her seeing red. How could he be so casual when she was so pissed off?

Grabbing the crumpled money, Bailey flung her car door open and rushed across the sidewalk. Her gaze was zoomed in solidly on Sebastian who was heading toward her with Mason fast on his tracks. They weren't laughing any longer.

"Is everything okay, Bay?" The worried tone of his voice did little to appease her. If there were something wrong, he'd probably just try to write a check to make it all go away.

"Fuck you." The words were tossed at Sebastian much as the money was, which hit him dead center in his chest.

Any trace of the smile he'd worn quickly slid from his face as the money pooled to the ground around him. Instead of anger, he faced her with a cool look, which only fueled her rage. "Good afternoon to you too, dear."

"I don't need your money, Sebastian."

"Yes, I can tell what a stand-up job you're doing of managing your life without my help."

"Alrighty then," Mason interrupted, looking between the two of them as if he was watching a tennis match. "I think this is my cue to leave. Hello, Bailey. Good luck, Sebastian."

"Do you want to discuss this rationally?"

"Rationally?" she parroted in complete disbelief. "I'm sorry, 'Bastian, but I'm not feeling very rational at the moment."

"Really, because you're hiding it very well. What the hell is your problem?"

"My problem is you treating me like some high-class whore."

"Whore?" Sebastian's gaze narrowed as he took a menacing step closer to her. "I've never treated you like a whore."

That was debatable. "You think leaving money on my bedside table doesn't count?"

"Are you kidding me?"

Frowning, Bailey crossed her arms over her chest. "What exactly about my demeanor comes off as a jest to you?"

"Bailey, you need a phone in your house."

"I have a phone in my house. My cell phone."

"Damn it, that's not the same thing and you know it."

"No," she shouted, not backing down. "I don't know it. A phone is a phone, and if the time comes when I can afford to reconnect my landline, I will. Me. Not you."

"That's fucking insane." With a grunt of frustration Sebastian spun away from her and shoved his hand through his hair, pushing it away from his face in irritation. He took a few calming breaths before turning to face her again. From the look of fiery anger in his eyes, the breathing exercise didn't help. "I have a great job, which luckily for me, pays extremely well. Your best friend is married to a man who has more money than they'll ever spend in two lifetimes. And yet you, with your stubborn-ass pride, won't come to either of us for help."

"If I needed help, I would have. Cat knew my phone was off, but did you think she presumed to butt her nose into my business and leave money on my nightstand?"

"That doesn't mean jack shit. Next to you, Catarena is the most stubborn woman in the world. Do you really expect me to just sit back and do absolutely nothing when I see you in need?"

"You just don't get it, Sebastian, do you? I'm not in need. I don't need your money. I don't need anything from you."

"You've made yourself extremely clear." His words were said with a steady calm so unlike him.

It took a bit of the bluster out of her anger, but not enough to keep her from going on. "Don't turn this around on me. You had no right to do what you did."

"Finally you said something I can agree with. Where you're concerned, I have no rights, no one does with you."

He said it as if it was a bad thing. "That's right."

"It's a stupid defense mechanism that's getting old. Sooner or later, Bay, you're going to realize the only person standing between you and happiness is you."

"I was happy before you."

"Liar." His accusation stung. "You know it and I know it. I make you happy and it scares you."

"Why would that scare me?"

"Because if you're happy with me now, you might be happy with me later. And later is what scares you most of all. I'm not some pretty boy who will be happy with a casual fuck every now and then. I want a real relationship with you, one where we more than likely will fight and love and fight some more, but at the end of the day we're still together."

Bailey opened her mouth then closed it. She wasn't afraid of a relationship with him or anyone else. Why would he say such a thing? Wait a minute, she stopped herself. He was totally getting away from the point and on purpose no doubt. "This isn't about me. This is about you and your stupid money."

"It's always going to be something with you, Bay. You're going to keep running, keep trying to find a reason to hide from me. It's getting tiring."

"Well, don't worry. You don't have to deal with it or me anymore." The minute the words flew out from between her lips, Bailey wanted to call them back. Everything seemed to go quiet around them as her world turned on its axis. Every ounce of her being urged her to take it back, to tell Sebastian she didn't mean it, but the hurt look in his eyes kept all her words at bay.

"If you believe this is how I think of you, maybe it is for the best."

Eyes wide, Bailey stepped away from him, hurt and afraid. He wasn't going to argue the point. Maybe he never cared at all. "Maybe we were better off as just friends after all."

"Friends…" Sebastian shook his head mockingly. "Were we ever really just friends, Bay? Friends trust each other, hell, friends like each other."

"I liked you." She even loved him, even though she'd never had the nerve to tell him. Now it was too late.

"Did you?" Without waiting for her to answer, Sebastian turned and walked away, leaving Bailey staring after him with tears clouding her eyes. She watched him until he opened the door and pushed past Cat, who rushed out, heading straight for Bailey.

Shaking her head no, Bailey held up her hand to keep Cat at bay. She couldn't handle her friend's sympathy right now.

"Bay…" The fear in Cat's voice propelled Bailey down the driveway and into her car where she started it and drove away, all without really seeing anything around. Damn him, he had totally turned everything around and instead of her killing him, Bailey felt as if he had killed a piece of her.

She didn't want to care about him. She didn't want to care about anyone, yet she couldn't get the wounded look in his eyes out of her mind.

Hurt and confused, Bailey did what a long line of Edwards women before her did when they felt lost—she ran to the safety of her mother's arms. Heartbroken, she sped all the way to the posh hotel Faye had reserved and rushed past a concerned bellhop to the elevator.

With tears streaming down her face, she knocked on her mother's door, praying she was in there and alone. The last thing Bailey wanted to deal with right now was one of her mother's suitors. To her everlasting relief, Faye opened the door alone, her smile instantly dropping as she took in her daughter's distraught state.

Without bothering to ask what happened, Faye welcomed Bailey into her embrace, pulling the sobbing woman into her arms as she cooed softly to her, "It's okay. It's okay."

"No," Bailey denied, burying her face into her mother's shoulder, feeling for the first time since Sebastian had left her apartment safe. "Why does it hurt so bad, Mom?"

* * * * *

In so many ways the past two weeks had been a living hell for Sebastian. It was hard not to remember the anger radiating off Bailey or the way her eyes shone with unshed tears, only her stubborn pride holding them back.

When she'd climbed back in her car and sped away from the curb, Sebastian had nearly followed her. Instead, he'd waited around, getting cussed out by Catarena. After the experience, he'd sat in his car down the street from her apartment and worried himself sick until she'd finally shown up sometime after midnight.

Getting home so late was reason alone to whip her ass and not the good kind either. For a few minutes after Bailey had closed her front door behind her, Sebastian thought about confronting her and trying to explain what he'd been thinking when he'd left the money. He'd needed for her to understand, to understand and accept his need to help.

He hadn't though, because at the time his anger had him feeling out of control. Even two weeks later just remembering how she could imply he'd leave money as payment for sex made him see red.

Hadn't he been the one insisting on more than just sex? Hadn't he been the one to actually show some emotion when it came to their relationship? And here he was being hounded not only by his memories but by Catarena and Faye.

Both women insisted he make it right. How could Sebastian explain he hadn't been the one to mess it up in the first place? He didn't want to go back over it with anyone. He'd been over it a million times in his head and each time he came to the same conclusion.

He was madly and passionately in love with a woman who not only couldn't trust but refused to love. Every time Sebastian thought about living the rest of his days without Bailey beside him, in his arms, in his bed, he ached so bad he was sure his chest would burst.

So he did what any self-respecting man would do. He worked himself into a stupor. The pile of folders littering the surface of his desk proved just how heavy a caseload he'd taken on in hope of forgetting.

Damned thing was, instead of forgetting as he'd hoped he would, Sebastian felt haggard and exhausted instead. But no matter what he did, Bailey was still there. In every breath he took, every dream he had, she made her presence known.

There was a soft knock at his office door. Without giving him time to answer, his secretary popped her head through the door. She'd been watching him with pity in her eyes for days. Women were damned intuitive creatures.

"Mr. Emerzian. She's back again, sir."

Sebastian didn't bother to ask who. He knew who she was. "She said she's not leaving until you speak with her."

His resigned sigh could be heard throughout the room. "Fine. Tell her I'll be right out. Thank you," Sebastian said before reaching across his desk where he began gathering the files he'd been working on. Once finished, he rose from his seat and made his way slowly across the room and out the door.

He might as well meet with Bailey's mother because if he didn't, Faye was never going to give him a moment's peace. She was utterly beautiful, extremely classy and as tenacious as a terrier with a bone.

"Sebastian!" Faye's gasp of surprise startled him. "You look as bad as my baby girl does."

Sebastian's first thought was "good". There was no reason why Bailey shouldn't be suffering just as badly as he was. But once his mind grasped the meaning of Faye's words, he pictured Bailey in his mind.

Her eyes no longer shone with happiness and instead of sassiness, she was bitter. The hurt written across her face would be evident to all. It was a horrible vision, a painful one.

"How is Bay?"

Even to his own ears, he sounded guarded. It was too much to hope she might come to him, to apologize or at the very least talk.

"She's hurting, just as you are. Can't sleep, won't talk and is cried out. How do you think she is?"

Sebastian heard the frustration in Faye's voice, felt it in every fiber of his being. "I don't know what you want me to say, Faye. Bailey made her choice. She made it very clear as a matter of fact."

He ran a hand through hair before continuing. "I know as her mother you don't want to hear this but Bailey isn't looking for a knight in shining armor. Hell, she isn't even looking for a relationship." And that was the crux of the problem as far as Sebastian was concerned.

They'd managed to muddle their way through his love for bondage and spanking but they couldn't seem to find their way past the label of friends, fuck buddies. The thought made him want to punch something.

"Getting angry won't solve a thing, darling."

"At this point, Faye, I don't think it can be solved."

Petite little Faye with her beautiful face and color-coded wardrobe turned into a mama bear right before his eyes. With her hands on her hips and a toe tapping, she laid into him. "I thought at least one of you stubborn-ass fools were smart enough to figure your way out of this mess but from the looks of it, you two couldn't figure your way out of a wet paper bag."

She pulled one of her delicate hands off her hip and proceeded to press the manicured tip of a finger into his chest.

"Now, you and I are going to have a sit-down lunch and talk this over. It appears neither one of you thought to figure out exactly why it is my baby girl has a fear of commitment. You damned young people. Always in a rush for the prize. You don't take time to enjoy the getting there."

Sebastian stood there staring at Faye. He tried to remember how many times Bailey said she'd been married but couldn't come up with the number. It was a bunch though, that much he did remember. Knowing she'd had so many unsuccessful marriages, Sebastian was a bit skeptical when it came to accepting her help.

"And you think you might know how to fix this because…" He let his words trail off.

"Don't sass me, young man. Now come on, we're going to lunch. Your treat."

* * * * *

Sebastian didn't remember much about what Faye said during the walk to his car or while driving to a local restaurant specializing in French cuisine, which evidently was a favorite of Faye's. It wasn't until they were settled at a table that they resumed their discussion.

"I'm assuming you know I've been married. Frequently." This was said out of the blue, making Sebastian choke on his drink.

"Yes, I do believe Bailey has mentioned it." What the hell was he supposed to say?

"I think it's because of my marriages that Bailey has a problem with commitment. Don't get me wrong, we have and always have had a good relationship. It's just she doesn't agree with my ways."

Faye stopped her explanation and took a bite of the salad a waiter had just placed before her. "Go on," Sebastian prompted when she was once again watching him.

"I guess you could say I fall in love easily, it's the staying in love I have a hard time with. And I have standards, very high standards. I like my men good-looking and with deep pockets. Many would say my attitude makes me a gold digger, I say it makes me smart. Smart enough to cover my butt at least."

Good grief! The woman was certifiable! No wonder Bailey didn't want anything to do with a committed relationship much less marriage.

"And all this has what to do with Bay and me?"

"She hardly ever went without as a child but everything she...we had was due to the good graces of whatever man I just happened to be married to at the time. It didn't take her long to figure out the hows and whys of it all.

"From the time Bailey was old enough to work, she swore she'd never let a man have the kind of power over her my husbands had over me. And she never has."

Faye stopped and looked at Sebastian. "You represent exactly the type of man, the type of relationship, Bailey never wanted to chance getting involved in. By leaving money on her bedside table, even though it was with her best interest at heart, you made her feel exactly as she did as a child."

Sebastian's heart hammered in his chest. He felt sick all the way to his toes and yet he was still angry.

"Bailey knows me better than that."

"Does she really, Sebastian? Has she ever truly let you in? Has she ever let herself go long enough to show you her true self?"

Sebastian wasn't sure he could answer those questions truthfully and come out ahead. Faye reached across the table and covered his not-so-steady hand with her own. "I see now you understand."

"I'm not sure I completely understand. What I am sure of is I'm going to do whatever it takes to fix things."

The trip back to his office after dropping Faye off at her hotel was spent planning. His head reeled with all she had shared with him. Sebastian now saw Bailey in a whole new light and loved and respected her more due to it. There was no way in hell he was going to give up on her but he needed help.

Pulling out his cell phone, Sebastian called Catarena. "Do me a favor?" he asked when she answered.

"No." Her answer was magnified by the click of the phone in his ear.

"Goddammit!" Sebastian cursed as he redialed the phone. He'd call again and again until he finally got what it was he needed. He would have his way in this if it took him the next decade to accomplish it.

* * * * *

Either Cat was the most insensitive person in the world or she had straight up lost her mind. Nothing else could explain why after badgering Bailey to go out so she could get her mind off Sebastian, Cat took her to the very place where Bailey and Sebastian had made love for the first time.

If she'd had any common sense at all Bailey would have never gotten out of the car when they pulled in front of The Boulevard in the first place, but Cat's promise that they would only be in there for a few minutes convinced Bailey to do something she instinctively knew she shouldn't.

Now she was fucked. Bailey should have just listened to the little voice inside of her head, although why she thought she was going to start listening now was beyond her. She didn't pay attention to her conscience when it warned her to shut up when she was arguing with Sebastian, so why was she so surprised she didn't listen now?

Standing in the doorway of "the room", Bailey stared doggedly at her soon-to-be-former friend, who surprise, surprise, wasn't meeting her gaze.

"What exactly are we doing here?" Try as she might, Bailey couldn't keep the hostility out of her voice.

"I'm meeting someone for some research."

"Research!" Hell no. Cat's words propelled her into the room as nothing else would have. They were not about to hang out in a sex club to meet up with some freaky-deaky master so Cat could get past her writing block. "Does Mason know we're here?"

Cat had the good sense to flush. "He didn't ask where I was going and I didn't tell."

Bailey crossed her arms over chest. That's exactly what she thought. Mason would have a conniption fit if he knew where they were, especially once he found out they had come without him. "So that would be a no then, right?"

"Mason is not the boss of me. I don't need his permission to do anything."

Bailey snorted at Cat's ludicrous comeback. Mason was so the boss of her and everyone knew it. "Let me just say for the record, I'm not going to jump in when he tries to spank you."

"In his dreams," Cat muttered crossly as she moved across the room and onto the bed still set up for display. "Besides, I thought spanking was more a you and Sebastian thing."

Bailey's smile slipped away. "There is no me and Sebastian."

Even saying those words caused her tattered heart to lunge in protest. It was a concept getting harder and harder for her to accept and what was even harder was knowing she'd played a big part in ending their friendship…moreship, whatever it was called. Labels didn't matter anymore. He used to be her friend. He used to be her lover. Unfortunately for her though, he was still the man she was in love with.

Hell, Bailey couldn't even sleep in her own bed anymore. Just going into her bedroom had her tearing up. She missed him. More than she thought was possible and it wasn't getting any easier with the passage of time. She was miserable and she had absolutely no idea how to fix it.

Stop it, Bailey. Get a hold of yourself. Shaking her head to clear her clouded mind, Bailey tried to focus on something else. "I don't want to be here all night."

"We won't." Cat sat on the bed. "So do you want to talk about it?"

"No."

"Well, I do."

"Then it's going to be a very fast conversation since you're going to be talking to yourself."

"Bay…"

Rolling her eyes, Bay joined Cat on the bed. She crossed her legs Indian style and rested her back on the headboard. She could be as stubborn as Cat when she wanted to be. "Cat…"

"I really think you need to talk to him."

"And I really think you and everyone else needs to back down and let it go. Sebastian and I will never work. I've accepted it. He's accepted it."

"What makes you think he's accepted it?" Cat asked, interrupting.

"Because he hasn't attempted to call me. Not once." And it hurt like hell. Bailey was willing to admit she'd been hasty, she was even willing to admit she had said a few things she shouldn't have, but she shouldn't be the only one knowing they were wrong.

"Have you called him?"

"That's beside the point." Bailey frowned. What was going on with Cat? Just last week she was on her side and now she had turned into a regular Benedict Arnold. "He hurt me, Cat."

"And you hurt him too."

"What did I do?" Cat raised her brow at her, sending Bailey a very pointed "you know what you did" look. "Don't look at me like that. The money was low."

"He didn't mean it the way you took it. He's not like any of your mother's men and you're not your mother. So why are you acting like an ass when you obviously love him?"

"Lot of good loving him does. Do you think he for once tried to see it my way?"

"Here's an even better question for you, Bay, did you try to see it his?"

"Look, Hurricane Faye Jr.," Bay snapped. "You're supposed to be on my side."

Cat smiled as she moved next to Bailey at the head of the bed. "You know what, this conversation has a familiar ring to it."

"What do you mean?"

"I mean, when Mason and I were going through the whole 'he's a controlling jerk' thing, you told me to give him another chance because I loved him."

"And I was right." Bailey so loved saying that.

"I just have two questions for you, Bay," Cat's expression turned serious as she stared deep into Bailey's eyes. "Do you love Sebastian and does he know it?"

Bailey broke the stare first. There it was. The very two questions Bailey herself had been wrestling with. The first answer was actually extremely easy. Yes, she loved him. She loved him with every fiber of her being. It was just unfortunate she couldn't answer the second question with as much certainty as she had the first one.

"Well, Bay." Cat took Bailey's hand in her own. "Do you?"

"You know I love him."

"But does he know?"

"He does now." Sebastian spoke from the doorway.

Startled, all Bailey could do was stare. She was in too much shock to do much of anything else. The amazing thing though, was Sebastian didn't look remotely surprised by her presence.

What the hell!

The bed moved as Cat began to ease off it. Bailey turned toward her former best friend, her mind in a complete jumble. Her confusion instantly cleared though, when she saw the guilty look on Cat's face. Well, that explained it. "How could you?"

"You kicked me out of our apartment, all I did was set it up so you guys could talk. I'd say we're about even."

"Not. Even. Close." Fury didn't come close to explaining how Bailey felt. She was going to kill her. Right after she killed him.

Deep inside, Sebastian knew Bailey loved him or at the very least had strong feelings for him, but to hear her say the words left him damn near speechless. The fact she was mad enough to spit nails didn't bother him in the least. How could it when for the first time in days, he felt as though things might finally be turning around for the two of them?

Sebastian caught Bailey around the waist when she tried to follow Catarena out the door. "Let her be, Bay."

She was pissed, kicking at him and all but growling in anger. She was absolutely glorious in her fury. "I will not let her be. I'm going to make her pay for setting me up."

His chuckle was low, almost too low to be heard due to the commotion coming from the hallway. "She'll pay, sweetheart. Mason insisted on coming with me."

Bailey stilled instantly in his arms. She cocked her head to the side as if she were listening. When she turned to him there was a wickedly evil little smile curving her mouth. "Good."

Sebastian thought things were going really well. Bailey was in his arms, even if not voluntarily, and her anger was aimed toward Catarena and not him. He remained in that line of thought until Bailey lifted her foot and brought it down on his instep. Blinding pain shot through his foot and up his calf. In his moment of weakness, Bailey was able to move out of his hold.

"Don't touch me unless you're invited to do so again or next time it might be an arm you lose."

Sebastian smiled, he couldn't help it. His foot throbbed and he might just lose an arm, but Bailey was in the same room with him and she was talking. It was a start.

It was time to up the ante. "I'll touch you all right. I'll touch you and taste you and roam every inch of your body with my fingers." Sebastian took a step closer to her. "And when you're ready to scream my name, begging for release, I'm going to turn you over my knee and set your ass on fire."

Sebastian took another step closer, grinning wickedly when Bailey's eyes narrowed. "Will it be a punishment spanking for stomping my foot or thinking so little of me you assumed I'd stoop so low as to leave money on your nightstand for sex, or will it be erotic, Bay? Maybe I'm going to spank your fine ass because I love the feel of your flesh beneath my hand."

Bailey's eyes were glazed over, her lids lowered. Every step Sebastian took closer to her only brought a deeper look of arousal to her features. Her nipples were puckered against the fabric of her blouse, making his mouth water. Sebastian couldn't wait to get through all the talk so he could spread her sweet thighs and taste the cream he knew would be dampening her panties.

When they were nose to nose, Sebastian leaned in close until their lips nearly touched and whispered, "Or maybe I'm going to spank you because I love the way you react to my touch, the way you let me be me without faulting me for my kinks. Maybe, Bay, just maybe I'm doing everything I've ever done with you and to you because I love you."

He swallowed her gasp of surprise with his lips. Tasting her again after so long made Sebastian feel whole and free, when only hours ago he'd felt as though the weight of the world was on his shoulders.

With his tongue, Sebastian traced the seam of Bailey's lips and when she opened, he plundered the warm depths of her mouth, dueling with her tongue, taking as much as she offered then insisting on more.

"Maybe that's why, sweetheart," he said, pulling his mouth from hers. "Maybe loving you is the reason for all of it, every last naughty thought. Every last dream."

"I didn't want to love you though, dammit!" She leaned into him, her arms wrapped around his neck for support. Sebastian couldn't see her face but he clearly heard the pout in her voice and when she lifted her foot, he thought for a minute she was going to stomp him again. Instead, she stomped her foot like the brat she was.

Sebastian pulled back, holding Bailey at arm's length. "We weren't given the choice, brat. It just happened."

"But you don't—"

"I'm so sorry." They both began talking at once.

With a single look, Sebastian won the right to continue. "I'm used to being pushy and taking control…even out of the bedroom." He waggled his eyebrows. "But I never meant to hurt you by leaving the money."

Sebastian led Bailey to the bed where he sat her on the edge before dropping to his knees in front of her. With a hand braced on each of her legs, he gazed deeply into her eyes, willing her to see the emotion he couldn't seem to put into words.

"I've never thought anything but the best of you, Bailey Edwards. Just knowing you could be so far off had me seeing red for a while, which was why I didn't call. I didn't plan to fall in love with you but I did and I'll never let you go."

"And do I get a say in this?"

She was going to be a brat to the end. The woman was stubborn to the extreme. "I'll have to hear what you've got to say before I decide whether or not your testimony is admissible."

Bailey placed her hands on his shoulders then slowly moved them up until she was cupping his face. "Ever the lawyer. What I want to know though is, who is the judge?"

"You're looking at him, sweetheart." When she ran her thumb over his bottom lip, Sebastian gripped it between his teeth and tugged.

"And this is fair how?"

Sebastian looked around him. He took in the large bed with its silky coverings as well as the rest of the room. The couch where Bailey and he had sat while watching Catarena and Mason. But tonight it was just the two of them, alone in the same room where not too long ago they'd learned the feel and taste of each other's bodies. How appropriate they were back in the same place when the circle finally completed itself.

"Because we're in the bedroom, Bay, and you know how I insist on being in control while in the bedroom."

She cocked her head and looked at him, her gaze intense, almost too intense. For a moment, Sebastian's heart raced. And then her soft and sensuous lips curved into a smile so brilliant he couldn't help but smile back at her.

"You're killing me, Bay." Sebastian levered himself off the floor enough that he could tumble them back onto the bed.

She giggled when he buried his face in the curve of her neck. "Tell me. Say the words to me this time, Bay, not to Catarena or anyone else. Me. Show me you forgive me for hurting you."

"Aww, 'Bastian. There's nothing to forgive. It was me. I am just so afraid I'll end up like my mother, owing one man after another, that I've spent my whole life afraid of loving."

"And now?" Sebastian gathered Bailey's hands in one of his. "Are you still afraid?"

She stared at him with tears glistening off her lashes. "Probably more than ever. The only difference is, now I'm not going to let it stop me. I love you, 'Bastian. Thank you for waiting for me."

She was his and never again would he let her go. Sebastian made the silent vow even as he took her mouth in a kiss so carnal it took every ounce of his willpower not to tear the clothes from her body and take her fast and hard.

"I love you, Bay."

Chapter Ten

ॐ

With three little words, Bailey's heart began to heal. It was the first time in her entire life she had heard the declaration from a man and believed him. Yet even though she trusted Sebastian loved her, Bailey couldn't let go of her past so easily.

Reluctantly, Bailey pulled back gently from his embrace and got up from the bed. She didn't want to fight but she also didn't want to pretend either. "As much as I'd like to act as if everything is going to be fine and dandy now that we've admitted we love each other, I can't. Real life doesn't work out that way. You're domineering, stubborn and entirely too sneaky for my peace of mind."

"And you're stubborn, spoiled and extremely stubborn," Sebastian added as he stood as well.

"You already said stubborn."

"I know. I just wanted to drive home my point."

"Smart-ass." Bailey smiled despite herself. God she loved this man.

"Bailey," Sebastian brushed her check softly with the back of his hand. "I'm well aware things won't always go smoothly."

"Or your way."

"Or either one of our ways," he agreed, ad-libbing a bit. "But I'd rather fight with you and for you than without you."

It sounded great but still Bailey felt the need to go on. "Money doesn't solve everything."

"And neither does running away." Bailey would have argued, if he'd been wrong. "I just need you to trust that I'll always be here for you and realize whether you like it or not, I'm going to want to fix everything for you."

"As long as you realize I'm not going to let you, we'll be just fine."

"Stubborn as hell."

Moving back into his arms, Bailey rested her head on his shoulder. "But you love me anyway."

"Without a doubt." Sebastian tightened his arms around her and Bailey felt as if she'd finally come home. The thought of home brought forth an even lovelier image to mind.

"Take me home and make love to me."

"We don't have to go home to make love."

Surprised at his words, Bailey lifted her head and looked into his smiling eyes. "You have a better idea?"

Sebastian turned her around until her back was flush with his chest and they were both facing the four-poster bed. Eyes wide, Bailey looked down at the dark blue comforter, which looked too familiar for her liking.

"You have got to be kidding," she gasped as Sebastian nudged her forward, his arms still wrapped around her waist. "You know how many people have used this bed."

"It's completely clean."

"How do you know?" Even to her own ears, her words didn't sound strongly like a "no". Hell, Bailey was all for making love with Sebastian again, it was the where and on what terms she was concerned with. Although the feel of him pressed against her, hard and ready, was definitely in his favor.

"Because I had Natalie ready the room for us."

Why wasn't she surprised? "So sure of yourself, aren't you?"

"No," Sebastian nudged the side of her neck, nipping gently at the tender skin. "I'm that sure of us."

The feel of his teeth biting into her skin triggered an instant reaction in her pussy. Before Sebastian, Bailey would have never dreamed of including a hint of pain with her loving, now she couldn't imagine sex without it. For the sake of false propriety, she tried once more, "What if someone comes in?"

"Then we'll charge a viewing fee and make them pay for half the room." Sebastian slid his hand up her waist and cupped her breast. Her nipples hardened instantly.

Her pussy gave a hungry clench as he tightened his fingers around her erect tip.

"Like that, baby?" Sebastian teased her taut nipple, squeezing tighter as she pushed her ass into his hard cock.

Bailey answered him with a guttural moan. It had been so long since she had felt his touch, she felt as if she could come from the sheer nipple manipulation alone. Fire raced along her spine as she squeezed her legs together, adding pressure where she needed it most.

Lucky for her, Sebastian was of like mind. He moved his other hand down her stomach and under her dress, pushing it up as his hand traveled her thigh to her very moist pussy. The feel of his hands on her skin was paradise.

When he brushed his hand across the wet satin barring his entrance, Sebastian growled. It was the only warning Bailey received before he grabbed hold of her thongs and pulled with all of his might. The cloth ripped, like countless other pairs that had stood in his way, and fell in tattered remains to the floor.

Sebastian didn't waste any time with pleasantries. He thrust a finger inside her heated core, frigging her as he held her to him. "Do you care where we are?"

"No." All she cared about now was getting him inside of her.

Instead of tossing her on the bed and ravaging her as Bailey would have loved, Sebastian continued to toy with her.

One moment he concentrated all of his attention on her nipple, keeping the rigid peaks at attention, and the next he was pumping his fingers into her hot sex. It was enough to drive a girl crazy.

Tired of his teasing, Bailey tried to bring her thighs together but Sebastian was having none of it. With a ruthless drive that was utterly maddening, Sebastian strummed her clit. "Do you care if anyone sees?"

"No." How could he possibly talk at a time like this? She just wanted him to fuck her and fuck her hard, but Sebastian seemed to have other plans. "Stop toying with me and fuck me."

"You ran from me, Bay. I can't just let you get away with that."

"Sure you can."

His deep chuckle had her creaming even more. The man was fucking lethal and all hers. "Oh I don't think so, Bay. You've been a naughty girl."

From the tone in his voice, Bailey knew she was in for a world of trouble. The thought made her smile. If this was his idea of punishment, Bailey was going to make sure she was naughty for the rest of their lives.

Sebastian's heart thumped wildly against his rib cage. Knowing Bailey loved him enough to open up about her fears and her willingness to work through them with him, together, aroused him nearly as much as the wicked twinkle in her eyes.

"So, you think you can handle what I'm ready to dish out, doll?" Sebastian added a little extra pressure to her clit, rolling the hardened nub between his thumb and finger, causing Bailey to whimper and press her ass into him.

"I can handle anything you throw my way."

"Mmm, sounds like a challenge to me, Bay. I say we do this the old-fashioned way then and see exactly what it is you're made of." He answered her challenge with one of his own, knowing damned well Bailey wouldn't be able to let it go.

When he turned her in his arms and stepped away, it was hard not to smile at the totally confused look she wore. Bailey stood there, just the way he left her, merely swiveling her head to follow as he made his way around her in a wide circle.

"What are you planning, 'Bastian? I'm not so sure I trust the looks you're giving me."

Sebastian stopped in his tracks. "You trust me, don't you, baby?"

Bailey stared back at him just as intently as he was looking at her. When she leaned in, licked his lips and whispered, "You know I do," against his mouth, Sebastian nearly came in his pants.

He had to take a reverse step just to get his raging libido back under control. The damned little minx was potent as hell. "If I do something or ask for something you can't follow through with, just say your word and I'll stop."

Her hip was cocked to the side, a sexy stance if there ever was one. Sebastian loved her sassiness and more than ever enjoyed the little skirts she favored. Knowing she wore thigh-high stockings beneath and not full pantyhose only increased the eroticism of the whole scene. Especially since he'd already ripped her little tiny, barely there panties from her body.

Moving closer to the bed, Sebastian sat on its edge. Her attention never wavered, following him every step of the way. When he patted his thigh, Bailey's eyes widened.

"Come lay yourself over my lap, sweetheart."

She moved toward him, her chin held at a stubborn angle. Sebastian wanted to rub his hands together in glee. There was just something about the upturned curve of a woman's ass—Bailey's ass—that made his pulse race and his mouth water.

Bailey sauntered across the room as if she didn't have a care in the world. The muscles in her calves flexed with each step she took. The sight of her breasts jiggling above the demi cup of her bra caught Sebastian's eye and held his attention.

When Bailey finally reached him, she slowly lowered herself until her face was damn near in his lap before scooting forward. "Like this, 'Bastian?"

The heated breath of her words shot straight to his cock like an arrow zeroing in on its target. "Oh hell!" The words slipped past Sebastian lips as a croaked whisper.

With one hand braced on his calf and the other braced on the edge of the bed, she levered herself up enough so she could look at him over her shoulder. "What was that?"

It was time to regain control. In order to do so, Sebastian slowly, inch by inch, lifted Bailey's skirt over the generous curve of her ass. "I said I'm going to enjoy hearing you whimper my name every time the flat of my hand connects with this pretty brown ass of yours."

Bailey was tense. Sebastian could only guess it was the anticipation radiating through her body keeping her muscles bowed tight. He rubbed his hand lightly over her flesh then followed the cleft of her ass all the way to the apex of her thighs.

"Is this all for me, sweetheart?" Sebastian asked, wetting his fingers before trailing them back up the cleft of her ass, delving just deep enough to tease the tight little hole of her back entrance.

Sebastian knew her heat and cream were all for him, only for him. Every word she'd spoken since Catarena brought them back together proved so. He kept playing with her because he knew it drove her crazy with lust. He talked dirty and asked silly questions he already knew the answers to because it kept her off guard, unable to concentrate.

Bailey used her hold on his leg and the bed to push back against him. Her groan of frustration when he pulled his hand away sounded conspicuously like a curse. "Ah, ah, ah," he tsked. "Why don't we do something with those naughty little hands of yours?" Sebastian paused, purposefully creating more tension by saying and doing nothing.

After a moment, he once again rubbed his hand over the smooth flesh of her ass cheeks. "I know. Why don't we tie them?"

It sounded like a damned good idea to him but Bailey's next petulant outburst made Sebastian think she wasn't so fond of it.

"I know. Why don't we just spank me and then fuck me and forget about wasting time tying me."

There was absolutely no way in hell Sebastian could hold back his laughter. She was just too much. Before his laughter died or Bailey could prepare herself, he peppered her bottom with stinging swats. Her gasps quickly turned into breathy moans as the heat spread.

Tying her hands was completely forgotten as he moved from one cheek of her ass to the other, making sure to cover each, to spread the heat. Her breaths quickened and soon she was panting.

Hearing his name repeated over and over in her sultry voice drove Sebastian on. He continued his erotic torture until Bailey gave him what he wanted.

"'Bas... Oh! 'Bastian!" His name blended together as she moaned, writhed and whimpered her need.

When Sebastian could stand it no more, he stopped the stinging swats and changed to light caresses. No longer able to hold back, he turned Bailey on his lap and took her lips in a searing kiss. It took nearly more control than he had to leave her be long enough to undress and don the condom he'd stashed on the nightstand.

There was no cautious touching or petting, only unadulterated heat as he finally covered Bailey's body with his own. "You're so fucking perfect," Sebastian murmured the words against her neck at the same time he kneed her thighs wide.

When he finally sank balls-deep into the fist-tight depths of her pussy, he knew there would be no leaving. "You're mine, Bailey. Mine," he growled as their bodies surged together again and again.

Sebastian surged deep, retreated then surged again, causing Bailey to come apart in his arms, quivering around his cock, milking him for every last drop of his essence and still it wasn't enough. He didn't want to let go, didn't want to leave the warmth of her body for even a second.

"All yours." With the return of her breath, Bailey whispered the words against his neck.

For the first time he could remember, Sebastian wanted nothing more than to leave The Boulevard and return home. This time though, he would be returning with Bailey in his arms and in his bed for the rest of the night.

Any commitment past tonight would have to wait. It was enough Bailey had finally agreed she was his and only his. It was a start Sebastian was going to grasp tight to and hold onto for dear life.

* * * * *

Philip was leaning casually against the bar when Bailey and Sebastian came walking arm in arm up the hall. From the looks on their faces, they had finally managed to come to some type of agreement.

Phil nodded and smiled as they made their way past him. Those two were meant for each other, just as Natalie was meant for him. He'd bided his time, waiting for some sign she was ready to move on with her life after being screwed over by her lowlife scumbag of an ex-husband. Only she hadn't shown any such sign. Hell, from the looks of it, she had no need whatsoever for a man in her life and because of such an attitude, Phil's patience was running short.

He surveyed the room, taking in the changes she'd made in the place. Phil knew if Natalie didn't ask for help soon, she was going to work herself into a stupor, if she didn't end up losing it all.

Revenue was good and she was getting applications for new patrons daily but it was costing more than she'd initially thought to get everything settled, leaving her in a financial bind. And because she was stubborn, she'd refused every offer of help either he or Sebastian had sent her way.

As if she knew he was thinking about her, watching her, Natalie stopped what she was doing and turned to look at him. The silky brown curls of her hair bounced around her shoulders and her big brown doe eyes looked even larger behind the frames of her glasses.

Phil couldn't remember ever seeing her without her glasses and wondered if she wore them because she needed them or because she thought they made her look less attractive. If looking less attractive was what Natalie was going for, she had messed up big time. Instead, they outlined her eyes and magnified the length of her dark lashes, making her appear even more exotic, even more beautiful, if it was at all possible.

Phil smiled and lifted his glass in a silent salute, drawing a frown from Natalie. It had been a long time in the coming but he finally had a way in, a plan to insinuate himself fully into Natalie's life.

His body tightened just thinking about the possibilities. He could already see the scowl that would cross Natalie's face when she got wind of his plan. Phil downed what was left of his drink, winked at Natalie and strolled out the front door. He could hardly wait.

Also by Maggie Casper

☙

Capturing Casey's Heart

Christmas Cash

Enough Love for Two

Maverick's Black Cat *with Lena Matthews*

O'Malley Wild: Hayden's Hellion

O'Malley Wild: Honoring Sean

O'Malley Wild: Zane's Way

O'Malley Wild 4: Tying the Knot

Tempting Tears

Tied and Tempting

Wicked Memories

Also by Lena Matthews

☙

Ellora's Cavemen: Dreams of the Oasis IV (*anthology*)

Full Exposure *with Evangeline Anderson*

Georgia Peach

I Never

Maverick's Black Cat *with Maggie Casper*

Myth of Moonlight *with Liz Andrews*

Seven Minutes in Heaven

Shadow of Moonlight *with Liz Andrews*

Stud Muffin Wanted

When Angels Fall

About the Author

৪১

Maggie Casper's life could be called many things but boring isn't one of them. If asked, Maggie would tell you that blessed would more aptly describe her everyday existence.

Being loved by four gorgeous daughters should be enough to make anybody feel blessed. Add to that a bit of challenge, a lot of fun and an undeniably close circle of friends and family and you'd be walking in her shoes.

A love of reading was passed on by Maggie's mother at a very early age, and so began her addiction to romance novels. Maggie admits to writing some in high school but when life got in the way, she put her pen and paper up. Seems that things changed over the years because when she finally decided it was time to put her story ideas on paper, the pen was out and the computer was in. Took her a while to catch up but she finally made it.

When not writing, Maggie can usually be found reading, doing genealogy research or watching NASCAR.

Lena Matthews spends her days dreaming about handsome heroes and her nights with her own personal hero. Married to her college sweetheart, she is the proud mother of an extremely smart toddler, three evil dogs, and a mess of ants that she can't seem to get rid of.

When not writing, she can be found reading, watching movies, lifting up the cushions on the couch to look for batteries for the remote control and plotting different ways to bring Buffy back on the air.

Maggie and Lena welcome comments from readers. You can find their websites and email addresses on their author bio pages at www.ellorascave.com.

Tell Us What You Think

We appreciate hearing reader opinions about our books. You can email us at Comments@EllorasCave.com.

Why an electronic book?

We live in the Information Age—an exciting time in the history of human civilization, in which technology rules supreme and continues to progress in leaps and bounds every minute of every day. For a multitude of reasons, more and more avid literary fans are opting to purchase e-books instead of paper books. The question from those not yet initiated into the world of electronic reading is simply: *Why?*

1. *Price.* An electronic title at Ellora's Cave Publishing and Cerridwen Press runs anywhere from 40% to 75% less than the cover price of the exact same title in paperback format. Why? Basic mathematics and cost. It is less expensive to publish an e-book (no paper and printing, no warehousing and shipping) than it is to publish a paperback, so the savings are passed along to the consumer.

2. *Space.* Running out of room in your house for your books? That is one worry you will never have with electronic books. For a low one-time cost, you can purchase a handheld device specifically designed for e-reading. Many e-readers have large, convenient screens for viewing. Better yet, hundreds of titles can be stored within your new library—on a single microchip. There are a variety of e-readers from different manufacturers. You can also read e-books on your PC or laptop computer. (Please note that Ellora's Cave does not endorse any specific brands.

You can check our websites at www.ellorascave.com or www.cerridwenpress.com for information we make available to new consumers.)

3. *Mobility.* Because your new e-library consists of only a microchip within a small, easily transportable e-reader, your entire cache of books can be taken with you wherever you go.

4. *Personal Viewing Preferences.* Are the words you are currently reading too small? Too large? Too… ANNOYING? Paperback books cannot be modified according to personal preferences, but e-books can.

5. *Instant Gratification.* Is it the middle of the night and all the bookstores near you are closed? Are you tired of waiting days, sometimes weeks, for bookstores to ship the novels you bought? Ellora's Cave Publishing sells instantaneous downloads twenty-four hours a day, seven days a week, every day of the year. Our webstore is never closed. Our e-book delivery system is 100% automated, meaning your order is filled as soon as you pay for it.

Those are a few of the top reasons why electronic books are replacing paperbacks for many avid readers.

As always, Ellora's Cave and Cerridwen Press welcome your questions and comments. We invite you to email us at Comments@ellorascave.com or write to us directly at Ellora's Cave Publishing Inc., 1056 Home Avenue, Akron, OH 44310-3502.

COMING TO A BOOKSTORE NEAR YOU!

ELLORA'S CAVE

Bestselling Authors Tour

UPDATES AVAILABLE AT

WWW.ELLORASCAVE.COM

erridwen, the Celtic Goddess of wisdom, was the muse who brought inspiration to story-tellers and those in the creative arts. Cerridwen Press encompasses the best and most innovative stories in all genres of today's fiction. Visit our site and discover the newest titles by talented authors who still get inspired - much like the ancient storytellers did, once upon a time.

Discover for yourself why readers can't get enough
of the multiple award-winning publisher
Ellora's Cave.
Whether you prefer e-books or paperbacks,
be sure to visit EC on the web at
www.ellorascave.com
for an erotic reading experience that will leave you
breathless.

LaVergne, TN USA
01 November 2010
203081LV00003B/136/P